The Blue Hen's Chicken

The Blue Hen's Chicken

Jewette T Battles

Writers Club Press
San Jose New York Lincoln Shanghai

The Blue Hen's Chicken

Writers Club Press
an imprint of iUniverse.com, Inc.

For information address:
iUniverse.com, Inc.
620 North 48th Street, Suite 201
Lincoln, NE 68504-3467
www.iuniverse.com

ISBN: 0-595-12678-2

Printed in the United States of America

In memory of my sister, Stella: Star "Aster"

Epigraph

Fate steals along with silent tread,
Found oftenest in what least we dread;
Frowns in the storm with angry brow.
But in the sunshine strikes the blow.

Crowper

Acknowledgements

I wish to thank my husband, Tom, and my sons, Leslie and Russell, for putting up with me and my wild ideas and dreams.

Most of all, I wish to thank my ninety year old Mama, Mary Thomas, for having such a terrific memory; my brother, Raymond (Bud) Thomas and his wife Bonnie, my "sister" for loving me. I love you too.

I would be remiss if I fail to mention my wonderful grandchildren Joshua, Megan, Jay, Justin, Catie; and to Doris, Tammy and Dinah for your love and support.

A special thanks goes to Bonnie Musselwhite for her guidance from day one, and to Frank Rueter under whose tutelage, I grew.

To my many friends who offered encouragement, I deeply appreciate your support.

Last but not least, many thanks to Gini Derrick for the last minute editing she so painstakingly provided.

Prologue

On the day of the girl's birth, the old Indian Will Sky, sustaining the custom of those descending from the People came to call. Gliding as smoothly as a floating feather, he crossed the front room of the shack and leaned over the baby's cradle. Gently placing his fingers on the newborn's tiny chest, he closed his eyes.

"What do you see, old friend?" Doctor Wilson asked.

"The will-o'-the-wisp."

Wilson's eyes narrowed in disbelief. *Illusion and deceit?*

Will Sky opened his eyes and inclined his head. In a soft, singing voice he told Ben and Effie Melton: "Nurture her gently with love; she will need to be strong."

A silence lay over the room until, in departing, the tiny silver bell that the old Indian wore on his belts—a symbol of his People's greatness—tinkled.

Dr. Wilson blew out, long and hard…"The Ignis Fatuus," he said. "The will-o'-the-wisp. Maybe you should call her *Willa*, Ben. It is a beautiful name."

And so he did.

Chapter 1
In the Beginning

"Oh please, Papa," he could still hear her pleading, "plee-eze let me marry Billy." For over a year, Ben Melton had wished a thousand times that he would have had the gumption to say no to his sixteen-year old daughter—and stuck to it. For the last few hours, due to circumstance, the memory clung to him, he reckoned, worse than stink clings to an overused outhouse.

In less than six months, Billy Rider had taken to carousing as if he hadn't a single responsibility. Then the fool—along with an idiot friend of his—tried to make some homemade whiskey. They rushed the process by cutting it with lye—dangerous business, especially in the hands of amateurs. Inside a week the lye had eaten their insides out. First the friend died, within days, Billy Rider, leaving Willa in the family way.

Now that it was October, cotton picking in southeast Missouri was pretty well over. But Ben Melton, having heard that a few farmers were still *scrapin'*, had risen before dawn, despite the inclement weather. Setting out on foot, he walked for over a mile before he found a sharecropper willing to hire him. Entering the field, he straddled the broken down row, bowed his back, and began pulling cotton bolls as if his life depended on it. When the pain in his spine intensified beyond endurance, he dropped to his knees and crawled. At midday, Ben paused only long enough to take two cold biscuits from the pocket of his overalls. Shortly after he finished his meal, the icy drizzle began to fall. Giving the bedraggled field a look of regret, Ben Melton shouldered his pick sack and headed for the scales.

The farmer weighed the cotton, told Ben he had to make a trip into town to the cotton gin, and offered him a ride. Ben was much obliged. Climbing onto the back of the wagon, he hunched himself down and, with cold-stiffened fingers, pulled the corner of the dirty tarpaulin over his head.

He heard the farmer lift the reins and prod the mules into action. At a gap in the fence, a click of the tongue drove the team onto Bone Road. Ben sensed the team balking when they were within sniffing distance of the warm barn, and he didn't blame them.

Riding along in patient discomfort, Ben solemnly stared as acre by acre of cotton, already picked, slid by. He had been told that every field within twenty miles of Hornersville had produced at least a bale to a bale and a half an acre. From the looks of the fields, he guessed it was true. He spat into the wagon worn ruts that passed under his feet and thought about how the change in the land had brought prosperity to some and devastation to others. Unfortunately, he was one of the others.

Ben's gaze drifted across the breadth of a cotton field to the new levee, bordering what was left of Little River. He calculated if God himself had come down and told him that they could—and would—drain The Great Swamps that had once stretched for more than 100 miles across southeast Missouri and northeast Arkansas, he would have been hard pressed to believe it.

At the turn of the century, commercial hunting and fishing in the wetlands—dubbed Swampeast Missouri—was big business. A steady flow of outdoorsmen, riding the rails from as far as New York City, poured into the area year round. From September through March, they hunted ducks, turkey, deer, and black bear. In the summer months, they fished.

Ben, along with his childhood buddy, Raymond Springer—whom Ben considered the best duck caller that part of the country would ever see—worked for a man named J. T. Beckhart, better known to the locals as Becky. Becky was a right colorful character, with his own way of talkin'. Those he hired to work the swamps, he called pushers; those that hunted, he called sports. As Ben's pappy, long dead now, had been fond of saying, Becky was the kind of man who could figure out how to make three nickels while everyone else was foolin' around tryin' to make a dime. "When I got too old to work," Pappy Melton would tell anyone willing to listen, "I took to sittin' under this here tree. But, old Becky, he up and started carving duck calls to sell to the hunters. In the beginning, they wud'nt worth dog shit for callin' ducks, but they was good mementos." Without realizing it, Beckhart started a tradition around Hornersville, one, which in time made him into a legend.

A slight smile twitched at the corner of Ben's normally pleasant mouth. They were good times all right; he had just started to call on Effie, his wife-to-be, and his friend Raymond was courtin' Vercie.

But things changed when they dug the diversion channel along the Ozark escarpment, cutting off Castor River, Whitewater River, Crooked Creek, and all the smaller streams that flowed through the Missouri swamps to eventually form Little River. The rich marshland was drained and turned into a series of ditches. The hunters stopped coming, and Ben lost his livelihood.

The farmer pulled the team of mules to a stop in front of Mays' Grocery. It took a few moments for Ben to snap out of his woolgathering and scramble from the back of the cotton wagon. As Ben's feet hit the ground, his body recoiled from the pain that shot up his spine, a result of the hours he'd spent bent over. Having grown accustomed to the discomforts of picking cotton, he simply winced and moved on.

The farmer slapped the reins and clicked his tongue. The tired old mules, anxious to get home, hunched their backs and moved on toward the cotton gin.

Limping across the road, Ben reached into his pocket and fingered the few coins earned, earned by his morning's work. He glanced at the pewter-colored sky and wondered, as he tossed his pick sack on the porch, if he'd make it home before the weather got any worse.

The radio was on in the store. Ben could tell by the announcer's excited tones that something wasn't just right. Being the kind of man who never liked to pry, Ben didn't ask any questions. Instead, he busied himself selecting a few staples, plus a treat for his daughter. Settling on a stick of chili fixin's and a bottle of Pepsi Cola, he placed them on the counter. He noticed Mays' hand trembling as he did his ciphering.

After checking his figures a couple of times, Mays scratched his bald-head and looked at Ben. "Sorry, " he said. "I can't seem to keep my mind on my business."

Curiosity finally got the better of Ben, "What's the problem, Luth?"

"The damn stock market's crashed, Ben."

"You don't say," Ben answered with what he hoped was a look of shock and concern on his face. He didn't know beans about no stock market, but he didn't intend to let Luther Mays know that.

Ben paid Luther, placed his purchases into a tow sack, and walked out of the store. He paused on the front porch, noting that the rain was changing to sleet. While he buttoned up his old, red mackinaw, he gave the weather a dejected grunt. With the pick sack draped around his shoulders, and the tow sack safely tucked inside, he turned down the brim of his wet fedora. Jamming it securely onto his head, he stepped off the porch.

Ben wondered what this thing they called the stock market had to do with him. He squeezed his pocket. He had fifteen cents left to his name, and it looked like it might be several days before he could get back in the cotton fields, if at all. He studied his hands. The burrs on the cotton bolls had made mincemeat of his fingers. "Can it get any worse than when a man can't even afford the price of a damn pair of gloves?"

In a matter of minutes, he was standing on Perry Hill, staring at the rutted path that led to the Holler. A line of bottomland hardwood trees marked the course of the once great river, sweeping off to his left and right as far as the eye could see. In front of him through the cottonwoods lay the Holler; land too closely tied to the river to hold any promise. It was a floodplain that no one laid claim to, squatter's land. Everywhere at his back were the cotton fields that had once been a wilderness, winter home to migratory waterfowl in countless numbers.

Slowly Ben descended Perry Hill, rounded the corner, and nodded to Joshua "Peg Leg" Snyder, like himself a one-time hunter and guide. Now Joshua was living in the relic of a burned-out car. Joshua never talked about the old times anymore, especially how he lost his leg in a bear trap. In fact Ben realized that Joshua hadn't uttered a word to him in over two years.

The wetlands had once been like a ripe fruit, and men like Ben and Joshua its harvesters. Didn't matter that you took from it every year; it'd always come back healthy the next. But instead of protecting it like you would an orchard, the government come in, drained it, and then cut it down. Ben turned and contemplated Joshua's demeanor for several seconds. Leaving good men ghosts of their former selves, stripped and discarded, ineffectual, like old peanut shells at husking time.

As Ben descended into the Holler and came to the cleared opening, he paused and dolefully surveyed the dilapidated shacks. Each a curious mixture of cheap lumber, scraps of tin, tarpaper, and brown brick siding. Perched on wooden stilts like birdhouses, Ben thought, in a futile attempt to evade the high water that was sure to come.

Ben didn't know who owned the Holler. Someone, sometime or other, told'em Happy Holler got its name years ago when the "Penny Cost Church" came down on the river and made the clearing. Word was they did it so they could sing, preach, and get the Holy Ghost as long and as loud as they felt like, without anyone up town complainin' about the noise they were makin'. Folks said they could still hear'em chanting their joyous redemptive hymns when the wind was right, so they took to callin' the place Happy Holler. That was long before anyone ever thought about livin' there.

Ben could attest to the fact that, during the winter months, happy days in Happy Holler were few and far between. Before winter was over, he knew from past experience, their steady diet of beans would gradually be reduced to more soup than beans. At the same time, the flour would dwindle. Effie would make fewer biscuits and thin the watery gravy until finally she'd declare, "You're gonna have to cross your legs this mornin' Ben. If you don't, this here gravy is so thin it'll mite near run right through you."

Worst of all, Ben knew some babies would die just for being born at the wrong time of the year—too tiny and undernourished from the start to keep warm, frigid from the second they popped from their mama's bellies until the little fellers couldn't take it any more. He wondered how many times this winter he would answer a knock on his door to find a mama cryin' and askin' him if he had a tiny pine box. It seemed he was always makin' tiny pine boxes.

As Ben trudged the path that snaked in and around the dilapidated shacks, he stopped and took note of a loose piece of tin on one of the rooftops rattling in unison with the pecking of the icy pellets. A scrap of tarpaper, barely clinging to the front door of another shack, picked up the rhythm, producing a primitive cadence. Ben glanced around. He had a most unnatural feeling. So much had happened to his family lately that he wondered—thinking of the old Indian, Will Sky. Then he forcibly shook his head to rid himself of such a bleak notion. He didn't believe in the supernatural or anything pertaining to Indian stuff; that was Effie's territory. But he couldn't shake the feeling that perhaps someone somewhere was trying to tell him something. Despite not believing as Effie did, he found himself hoping with all his heart that the unusual and hypnotic rhythms were a foretoken not of evil, but of good.

After entering the main room of his family's dwelling and shedding his wet clothing, Ben stood for several seconds in his drawer-tail, warming his sore hands over the wood heater. Slowly, he closed his eyes, knowing that when he opened them, they'd fall on the tiny crib in the corner of the room. Like a magnet, the crib drew him. He picked up the blue-flowered blanket Effie had made and pressed it under his nose, wishing with all his might that he could still smell the baby.

Though Ben Melton was a thick-chested bear of a man, at that moment he felt as helpless as a kitten. He did something he had always thought a real man never did…he dropped his head into his hands and cried.

On the evening before, Dr. Wilson had told him that baby Ben, his first grandchild, had died of congenital syphilis. First he must tell his wife Effie about the cause of death; then together they'd tell Willa that she too must surely be infected.

When Willa heard the news, she just lay on her bed and quietly sipped on her Pepsi Cola, toying with the faded quilt covering her knees.

"Papa, am I going to die?" she asked him so directly that it startled him.

Ben shook his head. "I purely don't know. Doc Wilson told me they got what he called a *kill or cure shot.*" Ben cleared his throat, dropped into the chair beside the bed, and unconsciously massaged his aching knees. "The Doc says the shot contains arsenic, and it can go either way. Anyone taking it has about a fifty-fifty chance of getting well." Pausing, he gently continued, "One more thing, Willa, he also said the shot is painful as hell to go through."

"I understand, Papa."

Ben reached over and took her by the hand. "Baby, he asked me about givin' the shot to you, tonight if possible. What do you think?"

Putting on a brave face, Willa said. "I don't see as I have a choice. So, Papa, you go tell him for me that I'll take that old shot!"

An ancient wail of pure agony vibrated through the room. Realizing that the sound had come from her, Effie turned her back and buried her head into her apron tail.

"Come here, Mama," Willa said gently.

The normally unwavering matriarch, who always knew what to say and do, collapsed onto the bed beside her daughter. Wiping the tears dripping from her mother's chin, Willa crooned, "Remember Mama, remember when I was a little girl and I'd hurt myself. You'd always kiss me first. Kiss me now, Mama," Willa pleaded.

Effie took a deep breath. With trembling hands, she caressed Willa, kissing her first on one cheek and then the other.

Blinking in a futile attempt to hold back the tears, Willa whispered... "You'd say, 'I'm the old blue hen and that makes you *the blue hen's chicken.*'" She gave Effie a little nudge. "Come on now, Mama, make me say it again just like you used to."

Gathering Willa's tear-stained face between the palms of her hands, Effie managed to choke out the appropriate words, ending with, "Say it, baby girl; say it with Mama." Without further ado, they gazed into each other's eyes and repeated, "*You can't hardly kill an old blue hen's chicken.*"

That evening, Dr. Wilson administered the carefully prepared shot. "Let me take the first watch," he told Ben. "It's going to be a long night, so you best try to get some sleep."

As Willa lay in the painful grips of the arsenic, Wilson gazed at the most beautiful young creature his old eyes had ever beheld. He thought of Will Sky's prediction on the day of her birth. "Fate didn't give you much time to glow, did it, Will-o'-the-Wisp, before it struck the first blow?" Wilson wished he could stay around just to see how life turned out for her. But, he knew, and he had known for some time, that his worn-out body wouldn't last much longer.

In the wee hours of the morning while Doc Wilson slept in their bed, Ben and Effie, holding hands, sat by Willa. From time to time, Ben Melton's shoulders shook in silent grief.

"Let's pray," Effie kept saying, "that the Good Lord won't put no more on us than we can tolerate." Each time she said it, she reached over and gently patted the back of Ben's hand.

The storm that had raged throughout most of the night soon passed, and the new day dawned bright and clear…a few hours later…so did Willa.

Chapter 2
The Way of Things

"Papa! How many times have we had this conversation?"

"I don't give a dang how many times we've talked about it. I happen ta feel like talkin' about it again, and I'm goin'ta say it to ye again. You need to stop dilly-dallyin' around and find yore-self another husband, gal, a good'un this time."

Willa scoffed. "A good one this time. Ha!" Snatching the remaining dishes from the breakfast table, she glared at Ben, and stomped across the sparsely furnished kitchen. The way she shoved the dishes into the pan of hot soapy water, causing the water to slosh onto the clean floor betrayed her annoyance. Grimacing, she hurried over to the basket of laundry and settled on a scrap of one of Ben's old shirts to soak up the spill.

"The last thing I need at this point in my life is another husband." Dropping to her knees, she gave the floor a couple of vicious swipes for emphasis.

Ben, who was bent over tying his shoes, raised his head, and cocked his good ear. "What was that you just said, girl?'

"Nothing, Papa."

Ben gave her a disapproving look. "Let me give you some more advice," he said, getting to his feet and walking across the room. "You best watch yore mouth."

"I'm sorry Papa." Though contrite, Willa was determined not to continue with this particular conversation. With a sideways glance at Ben, she bustled about the tiny shack, cleaning it as if her very life depended on it. If Ben was in one room, she made it a point to be in the other.

Ben watched his daughter's evasive tactics. She wasn't foolin' him for a minute; he knew what she was up to. Tenderness and concern for his only child, combined with the deep sadness he felt for what he had not been able to provide, softened his weather-beaten face. He thought about pursuing the subject but decided against it. He'd go run his trotlines instead.

Willa watched him go. She hated disagreeing with her parents, but her brief excursion into marriage had opened her eyes to the fact that a woman's role in life was mostly drudgery, especially in the Holler.

Willa moved about the hot cabin, working and trying to justify to herself taking such a resolute stand against her father's advice. Since it was wash day, she stepped outside, deciding to approach her mama with the *forbidden subject*—that of a woman's allotted place in life.

"There's wimin's work and there's men's work, and this here's wimin's work," Effie Melton declared as she bent over the rub board, taking out her irritation over Willa's independence on Ben's already frayed shirt collar.

Willa worked the handle of the pump, filling the wash tub with water. She eyed her mama. Though she knew it upset Effie to be asked these questions, she had no one else to ask. Certainly not Papa!

"Who says this is wimin's work, Mama?"

Hearing a clanking metallic noise, she turned to see Verna and Merna Higgers across the way, wrestling with an iron wash pot. The two young women, a couple of roly-poly identical twins, lived on the ditch dump with their husbands, Big Boy and Little Son Higgers, another pair of roly-poly identical twins. While the women struggled, the male twins sat under the shade of the cottonwood tree, in full view of the sweating women, without lifting a finger to help. Thinking, Willa surmised, about making their next batch of moonshine, or maybe about tarring a boat, which they would probably never get around to doing.

Willa watched her father cross the Holler and join the twins. "Look, Mama," she pointed to plead her case, in the direction of the men. "Even Papa is over on the ditch, sittin' with the twins under the shade tree, talkin' about God only knows what, while we do all the work. He could at least pump the water and fill the wash tubs."

"Don't use God's name in vain," was all Effie could think to say in return.

It's no use, Willa thought. She wondered why she even bothered. She gave an exasperated sigh. "I didn't use God's name in vain, Mama. You know that."

Effie did know, but she had felt compelled to say something.

It was all Willa could do to lift the tub full of clean water and place it on the wash bench beside Effie. She took a moment to catch her breath. Bending over, she used the tail of her dress to wipe away the perspiration that streamed down her face. It was a rag of a dress that she had altered earlier that morning in an effort to tolerate the blistering summer heat of the lowlands in southeast Missouri. Despite it being a rag, it accented every curve of her still-perfect figure.

Effie Melton, plain in her looks except for a head, except for a head of thick, dark rich hair, which she had passed on to her daughter, watched in admiration as Willa dipped her hands into the tub of water, splashing it over her face. Willa lifted her head and closed her eyes, savoring the reprieve as the deliciously cool water ran down her neck and over her breasts and arms, making her skin glow.

Deep down inside, Effie wanted things to be different, especially as far as her daughter was concerned, but she never expected they would be. Ben Melton was a good man. She knew how to get around him most of the time, but he was a man and so he believed a woman was meant to obey her husband. Regardless of how she felt about it, she didn't believe in planting false hope into Willa's head.

Effie sighed and bent her back over the wash board, rubbing a pair of Ben's *overhauls* with such vigor that she skinned her knuckles in the process.

"Here, Mama, let me do that for a while," Willa said and gently pushed Effie aside.

Effie gazed at her daughter with an uncommonly sad expression.

"I didn't mean to put Papa down, Mama," Willa whispered. She placed her head alongside her mama's, giving her a hug. "It's the way of things—as you put it—that I don't agree with. I'm just tryin' to make you see that it ain't fair. Why, Mama, Papa hasn't worked since cotton chopin', when you and I chopped right along beside him. We stayed in the fields just as long, and we chopped just as hard—then we still come home to do all of the work." Willa waited for Effie to answer her.

Effie didn't say anything; she just wrung out the clothes from the rinse water.

Willa was about to give up on her mama when Effie paused and took a deep breath. She let the shirt she held in her hand slide into the water. Placing her wet hands on each side of the tub, she looked at her daughter through keen dark eyes and spoke as clearly and distinctly as she possibly could.

"It don't matter how I feel about the way of things. So I'll say again, girl, it's *the way of things*. It ain't my fault, and it ain't yore papa's fault. That's all I can ever say about it. It's always been the way of things long since 'fore I was born. I don't s'pect for'em to change no ways soon. You best not either."

Willa snorted. She wondered who had made the rules. Not a woman, she was sure of that. She glanced in the direction of the ditch dump. After the mess she'd made of her first marriage, she couldn't imagine why her papa thought she'd be better off married again. The very idea!

Before her marriage to Billy, Maw NanEmmer Wilkerson had advised her, "Doin' it is for men to enjoy, not wimin." Maw Wilkerson had spoken only because Effie could not bring herself to talk of such matters with her own daughter.

Considering herself an authority on almost everything, Maw NanEmmer readily accepted the task. "You do it to mak'em happy, keep'em at home, and to have babies," she pronounced with an air of authority as she chewed on her willow stick dipped in snuff.

"Well, to hell with that!" Willa had thought from the first. With all due respect to Maw NanEmmer and her knowledge, she still wanted to know, "What about my happiness?" So she'd asked her friend Ruby Wilkerson—Maw NanEmmer's granddaughter—the very same question one day, reckoning Ruby knew more, given she had a sugar daddy in Kennett that supported her and Maw NanEmmer.

"If you really want to know what I think," Ruby said, her manner confiding, "most men don't know how to do it in the first place—the problem being that men have been as brainwashed about a woman doin' it as women have. In my opinion, men feel," Ruby deepened her voice and puffed out her ample breast, "if she ain't gonna like it in the first damn place, why in the hell waste time tryin' to make her? He just does his thing," Ruby laughed, "and then turns over and conks out for the rest of the night. The woman, she just lies there feeling cheated. Chances are she'll spend her whole life that way." Ruby took Willa by the hand. "But really, Willa, it's as much the woman's fault as it is the man's." Then she giggled. "Do you know any fine, upstanding, righteous woman that wouldn't die first before admitting she enjoyed doin' it?"

"I guess not," Willa grunted.

Ruby's manner changed. She fiddled with the red polish on her fingernails, trying to decide whether to confide something very personal to her friend. She concluded that Willa deserved to know. "Willa, honey," she said, "most of us don't enjoy doin' it because we think we aren't supposed to. I've learned something in the last few months. With the right attitude and the right man, it's a whole different ball game."

Willa didn't miss the dreamy look that suddenly appeared in Ruby Wilkerson's eyes.

"It's time you stop that day dreamin', girl," Effie said, interrupting Willa's thoughts. "We should've had the clotheslines full of clothes by now."

"Yes, Mama," Willa said. Lifting the tub of dirty water, she carried it to the garden spot, and poured it down the rows of potatoes. Then she rinsed it, pumped it half full again, lugged it over to the wash bench, and helped Effie carry boiling water from the iron kettle to fill it.

Effie added more soap and another batch of clothes from the soaking pot, bowed her back, and rubbed again.

Willa emptied the rinse tub in the same manner. As she stopped to examine the blister rising on her hand, she heard a burst of laughter from the three men still sitting under the shade tree.

"To hell with the way of things," Willa muttered as she carried the tub to the pump where she worked the pump handle, filling yet another tub of water.

The next morning, Effie Melton, after filling a basket with her prized homemade soap, set out for town, in hopes of either selling or trading it for staples.

"Mind you do the morning chores while I'm gone," she told Willa.

Willa watched her mama leave the Holler, wishing she could go along. Although it was early morning, the cabin was stifling hot due to the need to fire up the wood cook stove to prepare breakfast—no matter what the temperature.

She blew at the damp curls plastered to her forehead, took a deep breath, and headed for the kitchen to wash the breakfast dishes. After drying and stacking them on the open shelf above the cook table, she covered them with a clean cloth, knowing for sure that Effie Melton would have a hissy fit if she were to come home and find the dishes uncovered.

Even though her heart was not in cleaning, Willa rushed to finish her inside chores by first cleaning the soot from the globes of the two oil lamps. Retrieving the oil jug from behind the stove, she checked its contents. Since it was almost empty, she partially filled the lamps, saving just enough oil to fill the fruit jar lids under the legs of the pie-safe and the beds, a sure fire remedy for way-laying any friendly little buggers on the way to an all night feast. Setting the empty jug back into its place, she made a fervent plea to the Lord that Effie would have a good day, otherwise, they would soon be sitting in the dark.

Letting her eyes roam over the wood cook stove and homemade furnishings, she nodded in satisfaction. She'd done her work well.

"It's too god-awful hot to have to work," she mumbled. Hoping for a breeze, she pulled the flour-sack curtains aside. Leaning her elbows on the windowsill, she propped her chin in the palms of her hands and decided to search her mind for something pleasant to think about. "I know," she said. "I'll think about the dance that Arthur and Della Coleman are having on Saturday night." She sighed, and with her fingernail flicked at the last of the paint clinging to the window. When was Papa going to get around to giving her the usual lecture? For the life of her she didn't understand Papa. What could possibly be wrong with wanting a little fun in your life?

A sparrow flew into view, perched on the side of the cypress trough sitting under the hand pump in the back yard, and filled its beak with water.

"Hey, little bird, tell me something, since you travel the whole wide world. What's out there for me?"

The startled bird took flight. Willa heaved a sigh and decided to think about the recurrent dream she had been having for the last year. There was always a man, tall with blond hair—coloring so very different from her own. Placing her chin on her forearms, she stared after the bird.

Deep down she knew the man of her dreams would never be real. She blinked back the tears filling her eyes. Why would any man like the one in her dreams waste his time on her?

She thought of Justin Rider. Education, he always contended, is the key to life outside the Holler. "You can't get anywhere without it, Willa," he had said over and over. Willa sighed. She knew she should get more serious about educating herself. As her plain spoken mama liked to say, she hadn't gone to school long enough to know shit from Shineola before she up and got married. I'll think some more about it later, she promised herself. As far as she was concerned, she had done enough thinking for one day. Just so that she wouldn't feel guilty about not improving herself, she resolved that she was not going to say "ain't" anymore that day.

It suddenly occurred to her that she had not done the outside chores. Her eyes traveled to the moss-covered trough housing the precious cargo of butter, which Effie had acquired in a trade off with some sharecropper's wife.

She let out an exasperated sigh. Admonishing herself, she declared, "It's time for you to stop this bottle-ass'n around, girl. Get out there now, change the water in that trough, then lug in that wood! As if it ain't hot enough in here already." As she scurried out the door to the tiny scraped and swept yard, she corrected herself, "Isn't, damn it—not ain't." Pulling the plug from the trough, she watered Effie's hollyhocks, dumped the rest into a barrel for later use, and then pumped the trough full of fresh water.

Justin Rider, better known as Jay Sky, entered the Holler from the direction of town and called out to her. She acknowledged his greeting and watched her ex-brother-in-law and best friend cross the short distance in long, easy strides to the cabin he shared with his mama. He's such a handsome man, she thought. A good man, strong and intelligent. His older brother, Billy Rider, though good-looking, had been a no-account as Effie had repeatedly pointed out. Willa watched him shoulder the axe and head for the ditch dump. Jay Sky was the only person she knew who lived in the Holler by choice.

Hating the thought of going back inside the sweltering shack, Willa fooled around in the yard until she looked up to see the old Blue Hen a'comin'. She instantly remembered the pot of beans still soaking on the kitchen table, which she should have been boiling at least an hour ago. "Uh'o," she said. Gathering an armload of wood, she tucked her tail and scurried into the house, stopping only long enough at the back door to wipe the dust from her bare feet.

Chapter 3
In Disgrace

Willa was excited. She donned her best dress, brushed her hair, powdered her face, and even put on a little lipstick. Then she pinned a scrap of yellow ribbon that matched her dress in her shining dark hair. Feeling carefree, she danced into the front room to check her appearance in the long mirror.

Ben, who was at the table eating beans and cornbread, watched her. He softened. If it was possible, she looked more beautiful than ever. Almond-shaped, hazel eyes and high cheekbones inherited from Effie's Indian ancestors, then tempered by his Irish features, had produced a face of exceptional smoothness, the color of pure cream. Long luscious, chestnut hair floated around her graceful neck. Willa Rider could turn any man's head without even trying.

Ben had been aware for some time that Willa's popularity with the married men was a sore spot with their women. All day long he had been pondering what to say to his daughter about her conduct at the upcoming dance.

Over the years, Ben Melton, without ever formally accepting the responsibility, had become the unofficial peacekeeper of the Holler. He took his job quite seriously, even if it meant corralling his spirited daughter. He cleared his throat.

"Before we leave for this here dance, there's something I want to say to you."

Willa rolled her eyes. "What now?" she wondered.

"I want you to understand something bright and clear. I don't want to see you gitin' between a man and his wife."

"Papa!" Willa chided as she turned to face him. "I can't believe you just said that."

"Well, I did," Ben grumbled. "Me and your mama decided between us that it's high time we talk to you about it. You're rilin' up the men now, Willa," Ben said with conviction, "whither you mean to or not."

Tears glistened in Willa's eyes. She turned to face the mirror. "I'm sorry to hear that you think of me that way, Papa. I thought you and Mama, of all people, knew me better than that. There ain't…" she stopped to correct herself, "…I mean there *is not* a man in this Holler that interests me."

"It ain't what we think that I'm talkin' about. It's what other people *see*, and think they know when they see it," Ben answered.

Deeply hurt, Willa faced Ben. "What do you think they see, Papa?"

"Dammit all, girl," Ben said in a quiet voice, " they see their men gawkin' after you, and that's enough to git'em riled!"

Though Willa was irritated by the suggestion, she was intent not to let anything spoil her fun. "Ok, Papa," she said in reconciliation. "I promise not to get between any man and his wife. I hope that satisfies you." She pranced around the table, gave a little twirl of her skirt tail, and kissed Ben on top of his balding head.

Ben mellowed. "I know you don't mean nothin' honey, but yore far too pretty to suit some of the wives around here. I'm just askin' you to take it easy at the dance tonight, that's all. Rather than let you be the cause of a free-for-all, I'll send you home before the water gets hot."

Willa knew her father was dead serious, but since she didn't have any intention of starting trouble, she could not see the warning as a problem. Not a man in the Holler married or otherwise, captured her interest. If Papa didn't know that by now, she thought, then he wasn't any too bright.

Ben walked outdoors to wait. He rolled himself a cigarette and wondered if his little talk with Willa had done any good. He doubted it. He didn't like the restlessness he had seen in her lately. Thinking of one of Effie's expressions, Ben could see his daughter jumpin' from the fryin' pan into the fire.

While the family paddled down the river, Effie felt the need to add a few words of caution of her own. Troubled by the devil-may-care expression on her daughter's face, Effie ended her speech with a prediction. "Mark my words, girl, if you ain't careful, you're gonna fly around until one of these days, you'll land yore self right back in a pile of shit!"

At the dance, skinny old Whistlin' Pete Calhoun, sporting his handlebar mustache and bushy sideburns and smelling like Rose Hair Tonic, reared back in a straight back chair and picked his beat-up guitar. He kept time to the music by patting his number fourteen-size boots, from which a little toe with a big ugly sore protruded through a hole cut in the side. Every now and then, he spat tobacco juice at the spit bucket against the wall, missing more times than he hit. Ben Melton stood beside him, playing on his pappy's old fiddle.

Despite her promise, Willa was busy being sashayed around the dance floor by just about all the young men and even a few of the old. Ben managed a couple of good warning frowns, but they didn't seem to do much good. He reckoned she was gonna keep on until she had danced with every man in the house.

Willa knew her papa was watching—and 'er mama too. She really had intended to be good, but she loved dancing more than just about anything and simply could not resist the invitations to join in on every dance.

After a particularly energetic number, Ben announced it was time to take a break. There was a mad dash for the front door. Some were seeking fresh air, others a drink of whiskey. Willa took advantage of the rush to get away from Ben and disappear from sight.

Ben wove his way through the throng, not only looking for Willa, but also trying to keep an eye on the amount of whiskey being consumed. He had the men's solemn pledge that there would be no trouble. But pledge or not, he knew it wouldn't take much to get a ruckus going. If all hell broke loose, someone was sure to get hurt.

Willa wandered along the riverbank, ducking into the darkness when she saw her father coming. She knew that if she kept out of sight, Ben would eventually be forced to give up the search and return to the dance. Waiting patiently until he returned to the house, she moved from behind a tree, leaned against it, and listened until she heard him begin to retune his fiddle. She breathed a sigh of relief, slipped back onto the front porch, and settled herself against the railing to listen to the music. When she heard her favorite waltz, she jumped to her feet and hurried into the crowded room, moving as casually as possible through the people who ringed the dance floor. She was searching for Jay Sky. Not finding him, she assumed he must be outdoors, probably making out in the shadows. The woods were full of such couples. She had had more than her share of invites, but had simply laughed each invitation off and kept right on dancing. Yet when she heard giggles from the woods, she wondered why she felt so left out.

Willa was still wandering about when Rabbit Meaders walked into the party with a stranger. It didn't take long for the newcomer to spot Willa.

"Who's the good lookin' girl?" John Sinclair asked his new friend, Rabbit.

"That's Willa Rider. Her papa's the feller playing the fiddle."

"Well, I think you best introduce me to that pretty little thing, Rabbit," Sinclair said.

Rabbit shrugged. "Okay, but you're wasting your time."

"We'll see," the confident stranger replied.

He swaggered in a manner that suggested he considered himself to be God's gift to women. Rabbit reckoned that if Sinclair got anywhere with Willa Rider, he just damn well might be.

Willa had been studying the stranger from the moment he entered the house. To her he was, in a way, kind of handsome. As she watched, uneasiness washed over her. Normally, she wouldn't have given anyone hanging around with Rabbit Meaders a second glance, but she quickly laid those feelings aside because the stranger was looking at her. I can handle him, she told herself. All he needs to know is how to dance.

"Hey, pretty girl, how's about the next dance?" Sinclair asked her immediately after Rabbit finished the introductions.

Willa was excited to find that John Sinclair knew some of the latest dances and was willing to teach them to her.

"This is my lucky day," John whispered in her ear as they danced around the floor. "I just met the prettiest girl here and find out that she ain't married. How much luckier can a man git?" he asked, pulling her tight against him.

A little too tight, Willa thought, so she pushed him away. "Careful," she admonished him with a frown. "Luck has a way of changing."

"Promise not to dance with anyone but me," he said as he spun her around, caught her, and pulled her close again. "How about a kiss to seal the bargain?"

"Not a chance," she said and pushed him away for the second time. By now she knew without a doubt that John Sinclair would get totally out of hand given a chance. I should tell him to kiss off, she thought.

John was an expert at fooling people. His strategy was to back off when he needed to, wait, and then move back in for the kill. From the look on her face, he sensed he was moving too fast. He could see from her teasing smile that Willa yearned for adventure, so for a while he backed off and impressed her with stories about far off places about which she could only dream. Actually, he had not traveled himself, but he knew she wouldn't know the difference, and he was right.

Before long, John talked Willa into going outside for some fresh air. They joined a group and without hesitation, John reached for the bottle of moonshine being passed around. He took a swig and offered the bottle to Willa.

"No, thank you. I don't drink," she stated. The uneasiness she had stifled earlier in the evening surfaced.

"Awe come on, honey," John coaxed, his voice going up a notch, "one little drink never hurt nobody. It'll make you feel good."

Everybody laughed and agreed with John.

"Didn't you just tell me you needed a little fun in yore life? Here's yore chance," he wheedled.

Willa had such a desperate ache in her soul to end the loneliness that had plagued her for so long, she threw caution to the wind.

"Have some more," he said when she had had enough.

Woozy and hardly able to stand on her own two feet, she let John steer her toward the woods.

His face became hard and callous as she stared into his eyes. "I'm going to hump the hell out of you, you little teasin' bitch, right here and now, and there ain't a damn thing you can do to stop me."

Before she could protest or resist, he thrust her roughly up against a tree, smothering her mouth and stifling her protests with his harsh, bristled face.

The next morning the dull ache between her legs, the bruises on her inner thighs, plus the hide rubbed from her spine were constant reminders of the brutal assault she endured the night before.

It rained all day without a single break, the day she admitted to herself, and then to Ben and Effie, that she was pregnant. She read the disappointment in their eyes and ached to tell them how it really happened. If she did, she knew her papa well enough to know he'd up and kill John Sinclair.

It didn't take long for the news of Willa's disgrace to cover the Holler. Some of the women felt compassion for Willa, and some allowed that she got what was comin' to her, parading herself around like she did.

Maw NanEmmer put in her two-cents worth by reckoning they had all better clean out from under their own door steps before they started cleanin' out from under Willa's. Maw's rheumatism had her down, so she sent word by Ruby her granddaughter, for Willa not to worry. It was going to be all right, and for Willa to remember that there ain't nothin' new under the sun.

Ruby didn't know what Maw meant by it. She simply related the message and hoped Willa could figure it out. Despite the situation, Willa had to laugh. Whatever it meant, Willa knew Maw meant well. She told Ruby to thank her for the kind words.

John Sinclair was quietly told in no uncertain terms just how the ball bounces in the Holler. As the Higger twins put it, sometimes the old ball bounces right into the river. "An' it ain't ever heerd from again, if you get the drift."

"But I don't want to marry him, Mama," Willa cried.

"You got no choice, girl," Effie kept saying. "No woman does once she gets herself in trouble."

The normally fastidious Willa stared at the disheveled reflection of the wounded soul in the mirror and could not believe it was she. She lifted her hand to undo the hair carelessly knotted at the nape of her neck. Instead, she pulled at the tangled strands that hung haphazardly about her face and wondered how she had let this happen to her. Effie's words came back to haunt her. She had definitely landed in a pile of shit all right, one from which she couldn't get out.

She leaned into the mirror to study the dark circles under her eyes and realized for the first time in her life, she didn't care how she looked. She tossed the hairbrush onto the dresser and simply refused to change her appearance. Closing her eyes, she tried to squeeze back the tears. "Mama, Mama," she cried in desperation. How she wanted to crawl into Effie's arms. Nothing in this world made sense. She was in disgrace. Adultery and infidelity was nothing new in the Holler. Why was getting pregnant without the benefit of matrimony considered more of a sin than the act itself? Surely, God doesn't see it that way. It seemed to Willa, at this moment in her life, that everything in the world was ass backwards. But it didn't matter how she felt about anything anymore. She considered herself doomed to the life of the Holler. She'd grow old before her time, like all the other Holler women, having babies, working all day in the fields to feed them, then going to bed at night, which usually ended up with making more babies.

Willa's eyes hardened with determination. "Don't you forget, not even for a minute, Willa Rider, you're the old blue hen's chicken." She picked up the hairbrush and pounded it on the dresser. Leaning forward, she looked herself in the eyes and made a vow. "I have no choice but to marry that sonofabitch! But I promise here and now, there will be no pleasure in my bed for him, now or ever!"

Chapter 4
In This Manner

St. Louis, Missouri. Young Robert Vaughn awoke to find that he was in jail. Partly due to the horrendous hangover he was experiencing, he was only mildly curious about what he had done to get there. Hearing a noise, he looked up to see an uniformed guard unlocking the door.

"Mind telling me what I did this time?" he asked.

The officer's eyebrows shot up. "You don't know?"

Robert raised himself up and rubbed his hands down his face. "Hell no, I don't know. If I did, why would I be asking?"

Taking note of the sarcasm in the young doctor's voice, the officer decided not to tell him. "Frankly, I don't know either," he said. He escorted Robert down the hall into a waiting room where he left him to cool his heels.

Robert dropped onto the worn-out sofa. Hoping to grab a few winks, he made himself as comfortable as possible. Before he dozed off, he thought about his situation. Without much effort, he came to the same conclusion he always did when he was in trouble—he didn't give a rat's ass.

After being bailed out, later that day he sat in his father's office. "Do you think I am going to use my influence to get you out of it this time?"

Vaughn Senior bellowed. He raised himself from his chair, and for emphasis, brought his fist down with a thud in front of Robert's pounding head.

Robert winced, but kept his mouth shut. Funny, the only emotion he could ever remember his father displaying toward him was rage.

Harrison Vaughn was an older version of his son, except that his once lean body had thickened around the middle and his sandy-colored hair was now streaked with gray. He still retained his piercing, sky-blue eyes and knew how to use them to his advantage. As far as both men were concerned, any resemblance of the two was a mere matter of externals.

Vaughn Senior eyed his son. Who in the hell does this young whippersnapper think he is? He can't even get his head out of his ass long enough to see that the whole world is on it's way to hell. He's never suffered a day in his life—at the same time the rest of the country is in the midst of a depression with millions of people out of work. Jamming his hands into his pockets, Harrison Vaughn walked over to the window and stared down at the parking lot. For the life of him, he could not understand this boy.

Had Robert been privy to his father's thoughts, he would have agreed. His father did not understand, nor had he ever understood, the least of Robert's needs.

Vaughn Senior's voice droned on, but Robert didn't pay much attention, until the mention of his mother. Robert shut his eyes at the sound of her name.

"I'm not leaving you, Robby," he could still hear her say. "I'm only going to the hospital. *Don't worry about me, I'll be back.*"

Eight years old at the time, Robert never saw his mother again. He wasn't even allowed to attend the funeral. His father thought it best. In a matter of days, he was shipped off to a boarding school. It was several agonizing months before he understood what had happened. Hell! When had his father ever known what was best for him?

"If this should go to trial, Robert, do you know what it will do to your career?"

Robert didn't bother to answer. Instead, in his mind he echoed each word his father uttered because he had heard them all before.

Harrison Vaughn paced back and forth. He didn't have time for this. He was in the midst of some very important work that needed his full attention. What this boy needs is to be taught a good hard lesson. Recently, he had learned that the southeast part of the state was begging for a doctor. It's time his boy stood on his own two feet.

Robert slouched in his chair. Extending his feet under the desk to make himself more comfortable, he let his eyes follow his father around the room, hoping this wouldn't last much longer. His head ached and his eyes burned from the lack of sleep. Besides, he was bored with the whole thing. All it takes, he thought, is money, old man, and it will all be over. Money is the magic word nowadays. He tried to hide the smirk that was formed on his face.

His father turned, catching the sneer on the young whelp's face. The old man's eyes hardened. This matter is settled.

Robert sat in silence as his father gave him an ultimatum: either face the law and pay through the legal system by going to jail, or agree to leave St. Louis and serve for five years as a general practitioner in the Missouri bootheel.

Jesus, Robert thought, the bootheel! As far as Robert was concerned, his father just wanted to get rid of him. He knew, and he had known for many years, that the research department at Barnes Hospital was more his father's child he felt, than he had ever been.

On the day before the reckoning, without a word to his father, he climbed into his car and headed south, letting the rage he had nursed since a small boy burn into his very soul.

Chapter 5
Against His Wishes

Hornersville, Missouri. Robert pulled the car to a stop and glanced up at an old two-storied Greek revival house, which might have had character if it hadn't been in such dire need of paint. A sign hanging on the door read, "Hotel, Rooms for Rent." On the other side of the street, clinging and clanging was the cotton gin. To the left of the gin sat a round contraption for burning cotton hulls, which belched smoke, covering everything with a thin shroud of gray. After wiping the sweat from his face, he drove across the railroad track and into town.

The mayor had written him that both the mayor's office and the doctor's office were located on Main Street, and that the main street of the town ran north and south. Being a true city dweller, Robert automatically checked the street sign. The sign pointing north and south read Mound Street instead of Main. The one pointing east and west read Main Street. Since it was his understanding that the office he was to occupy was on Main Street, he turned west. He couldn't see a thing but some run-down old houses and at least a dozen kids playing up and down the block. "They should call this street Kid Row," he muttered. "If the damned doctor's office is on this street, I'm sure as hell heading out of here." He made a right turn and suddenly found that he was in the middle of the cotton ginning operation.

"What the hell does that idiot think he's doing?" one cotton farmer complained to another as Robert maneuvered his car through the wagons, spooking the mules in the process.

Back on Mound Street, he drove past three pool halls, several grocery stores, a restaurant, a dry goods store, and a five and dime. A rickety gas station sat on the corner across from the flagpole, proudly flying Old Glory. He spotted the doctor's office, an old converted house that needed painting. He could barely make out the name—Dr. Frank Wilson, M. D. —on the faded shingle hanging out front. Across from the office sat the post office, hardware, theatre, and bank. At the end of the street, he made a U-turn to park in front of the City Hall. Across the street in a rundown building with steam hissing out of its side was Gossett's Dry Cleaners.

James Horner Shaw, attorney-at-law, watched from across the street. Observing the young man's dissipated countenance, Shaw judged him to be haughty. This opinion was reinforced by the city slicker's attention to his obviously new Speedster Runabout. "This must be our new M. D.," James surmised. He watched as Robert walked around the car. He looks to be somewhat of a pompous jackass; he thought, then turned and went back to his work.

Robert grimaced when he saw that all four tires of his new Packard had manure embedded in them. As he reached to open the door to the office of the City Hall, he glanced up at what had been a deserted street to see several knots of people staring in his direction. He stared back until his hand touched something sticky. He shifted his gaze, and then he jerked his hand back from a gummy piece of paper completely covered with the carcasses of dead flies. Robert closed his eyes, reached into his pocket for his handkerchief, and delicately wiped at his fingers. Cautiously, so he wouldn't touch the thing again, he opened the door.

Marshal Cleve Cushman sat leaning back in the Mayor's chair. He had his feet on the desk and a spit can by his side. An electric fan, positioned just right, blew full into his red face. He had a Lone Ranger comic book propped between his knees and his fat belly. At the sound of a car pulling up in front of the building, Cushman glanced out the window, hoping to hell that it wasn't someone wanting him to do something. The old swivel chair let out a loud groan as the marshal slowly rose and ambled over to meet the well-dressed stranger. He rubbed his hand on the side of his leg as if to clean it before he stuck it out to Robert in a greeting.

"Howdy," he said through the chaw of tobacco filling his mouth. "I'm Cleve Cushman, the marshal." A thought suddenly occurred to him. He squinted at Robert. "You wouldn't be the new doc, would'che?"

"I'm afraid so," Robert said, wiping the perspiration from his forehead. "Is it always this damn hot down here?"

"Only in the summer," Cushman snickered.

Robert was in no mood to be ridiculed. He felt like knocking the hell out of the fat smart-ass.

"The Mayor ain't here right now, cause we didn't expect ya' until tomorrow," the lawman stated. "He's got the grocery store across the street yonder by Lawyer Shaw's office."

Robert sighed and reached for the door handle.

Cushman hunched his backside onto the corner of the desk. "But he ain't there either," he said.

Robert let go of the door. "Then where in the hell is he?" he asked in exasperation.

"Him and Bob Vendells gone up to Kennett, the county seat. I reckon on some kind'a city business. He'll be disappointed he didn't get to greet you. He was plannin' on showin' you around and have'n a big to-do."

"Thank God I came today," Robert muttered under his breath.

The marshal rummaged around in the desk drawer. "Here's the keys to yore house and the doctor's office," he said. He pitched them onto the desk in front of Robert. A frown crossed his face as the realization finally soaked in that the doctor would need some assistance to get to his new home, which meant he was going to have to get out into the heat.

"I reckon if you'll follow me I'll show you where yore house is," he added, without much enthusiasm.

You're not only a smart-ass but a lazy-ass as well, Robert thought as he followed him out the door.

The marshal eyed the Runabout. He gave the front tire a couple of kicks. "Some car you got there, Doc. Don't reckon I ever seen one like it. What kind is it?"

"It's a Packard."

The marshal walked over to the old beat-up Model T patrol car, opened the door, and leaned on it as he spoke. "It's too damned hot out to do much sight seein', but if' you want, I'll take you around in a day or two. That is, if' that's all right with you?" He didn't want the mayor coming down on him for not doing right by the new doctor.

Robert glanced at the front tires on his car, wondering what more there might be to see. He felt as though he had just taken the grand tour all by himself. He raised his eyes to take another look down Mound Street. "That will be more than fine with me, Marshal. Right now, all I want is a cool place and a cold drink."

Cushman looked relieved. He worked hard at doing nothing more than necessary to keep his job, especially if it meant moving around in the heat.

Bothered by something he didn't understand, Robert shook his head. He raked his hand through his hair. He just had to ask. "Why is the main street of this town on Mound Street?"

His question drew a blank expression on Cushman's face. No one had ever asked him that before, and he didn't rightly know.

Cushman circled the flagpole, and headed down a side street. He traveled for about two blocks before turning into the drive of a cottage-style house.

Robert later learned that it had belonged to his predecessor, Dr. Wilson. The house proved to be the best thing he had seen all day. He arrived here with visions of living in the back of the doctor's office.

The cottage was a fairly good-sized structure with three bedrooms, a living room, dining room, and large old-fashioned kitchen. There was a huge screened-in back porch and a front porch with round white columns. On the front porch sat two white rocking chairs. A quick peak around the corner revealed a fenced back yard, well shaded by a massive oak tree.

Robert thanked the marshal and entered the house. The moving van with his belongings had been shipped in advance of his arrival. As he walked through the house, it was obvious that the women folk took control of arranging his furnishings and preparing the house. In the hallway he flipped the switch to a giant attic fan. The whirlwind breeze circulated through the house providing a coolness that soothed his hot, weary body and his bruised soul.

Just off the master bedroom, Robert found the bathroom. He breathed a sigh of relief that the house had one. Dominating the center of the exterior wall next to a small window sat a large-footed, granite bathtub with a shower. Fresh towels hung on wall pegs beside it. He really didn't know how lucky he was. Most of the town didn't have running water, let alone a bathtub and inside toilet.

Robert paid little attention, if any, to the rest of the house. He paused only long enough to check the condition of his mother's furniture, crystal, and silver that had been in her family for several generations. He didn't care about the rest of the house. As far as he was concerned, it was a prison. If he could manage it, he would be gone before the five years were up. If that old man of his thought he was going to stay buried in this hick town, he had another thought coming.

After placing his luggage in the master bedroom, he went into the kitchen, hoping to find ice in the refrigerator. Not only did he find ice, but he also found the icebox stocked with food. The sight and the feel of the ice were the only thing that made the slightest bit of an impression on him right now. The kindness of the local ladies who worked with such special care to make their new doctor's home welcoming and comfortable was completely unappreciated by him.

He set the bottle of whiskey he'd brought from St. Louis onto the table. Breaking some ice loose from the ice tray, he dropped three cubes into a tall glass and poured the glass half full of whiskey. Then he filled it to the top with water. Robert allowed the drink to cool before taking a big slug, which both cooled and warmed his body as he drank it down. Taking his drink to the bathroom, he stripped and indulged in a cool shower.

Then Robert Harrison Vaughn, M.D., one of the prestigious Vaughns of St. Louis, Missouri, dropped onto the hundred-year-old bed that had been in his mother's family for generations, and there he lay in perfect misery. For the rest of the afternoon, he forced himself to rise only long enough to replenish his whiskey. As he finally drifted into a fretful sleep, in the back of his mind arose the small hope that when he awoke, this experience would prove to be a bad dream.

Chapter 6
Under the Name of Penalty

Willa Sinclair straightened her aching body and gazed across the field of waist high cotton, white as far as she could see. Down the mile-long rows, waves of heat danced in frenzy. At the moment, the cotton wagon seemed a long way off.

Ben took his hat off and reckoned to his daughter that hell couldn't be any hotter than a cotton patch in August. He wiped the sweat from his eyes onto the sleeve of his faded work shirt and watched as a dozen or more heads in droopy bonnets and sweat-soaked hats popped up intermittently to stretch their backs.

Willa heard a grunt and looked behind her where a man was in the process of picking up a sack full of cotton. He staggered a few times, bowed his back, and bucked the sack to balance it across his right shoulder and arm. When he passed, he grunted out a "howdy" and moved on. Ben and Willa said "howdy" back and watched him repeat his balancing act at least four more times before reaching the wagon. Inside of the cotton wagon, Ben and Willa could see the farmer, Uncle Jim Harden, wearing a dilapidated straw hat, methodically tromping the cotton down to make room for more.

By the time Willa reached the dividing point halfway down the mile-long rows, she was completely exhausted. She breathed a sigh of relief and ran her fingers under the worn strap of the heavy pick sack that bit deeply into her shoulder. She readjusted it, trying to find a spot that didn't hurt. With Ben's help, she dragged the sack across the rows to the scales to be weighed by the farmer.

While Ben tended to the cotton, Willa dropped beside the wagon wheel into the only available shade in the entire field. She pulled the faded bonnet from her head and fanned herself. Resting her back against the wheel, she closed her eyes, praying for some relief from the heat.

"You got sixty-two pounds of cotton here, Ben," Uncle Jim announced.

Ben took his sack away and tossed it into the wagon. He hung Willa's in its place. With the farmer's help, Ben emptied the sacks and then climbed down from the wagon.

The next thing Willa knew, Ben dropped down beside her. He took a crumbled piece of paper from his pocket along with a stub of a pencil. Touching the end of the pencil to his tongue, he did some reckoning, "That makes me over two hundr'd and twenty pounds for the day. You had forty-five pounds, which makes you a hundr'd and seventy-two pounds."

Willa didn't say anything. She just barely lifted her head enough to acknowledge Ben's comment.

Ben took a drink from the water jug and studied Willa's face. He noticed the lines of fatigue around her eyes. "You're feeling bad, ain't ye, Hon?"

Willa opened her eyes. She didn't think she had the energy to lift her head. She let it roll to one side and looked at Ben. "No, Papa," she lied.

"I'm worried about you, just the same," Ben continued. "You ain't been actin' right lately. While we're making a little money, why don't you go see that new doctor they been talkin' about?"

"I don't need to see a doctor, Papa." Willa said in a tired voice. "Besides, I don't have the money to spare. I'm going to need every dime I make to buy food to carry us through the winter."

"That damn John ouht'a be out here pickin' cotton with'ya."

Willa snorted. "Tell me about it, Papa." She ran her hands through her damp hair. "I'm sorry," she said, "I can't force him out here, no more than you can."

"I know it," was all Ben said. He had a lot more he'd like to say about John, but he knew it would be a waste of time. He looked at his aged pocket watch. "We got jest about enough time to finish these rows before going home." He pulled himself to his feet and took Willa's hand to help her up. She felt the squeeze before he released it. "You know all you have to do is say the word, and I swear to the Good Lord, I will see him packin'. You and the baby can move back in with me and yore mama."

"And be a burden on you?" She shook her head.

Ben saw tears even though she tried to hide them.

"No, Papa. As Mama would say, I made my bed, so…" she sighed, "I guess I'll just have to lie in it."

The sun was completely gone from the sky by the time Ben and Willa rode the cotton wagon into town and walked the rest of the way to the Holler. Willa hung the patched pick sack on the side of the shack. Walking to her mama's house to get the baby, she took solace in the fact that hopefully John would not be at home when she returned. With Aster planted firmly on her hip, she climbed the steps and wearily opened the front door of the dingy little shack she had also lived in with Billy. Lighting the oil lamp, she glanced around for John. Thankfully he was nowhere in sight. But John was seldom around except to sleep off a drunk.

Placing Aster on the floor by the door, she said, "Don't move."

Aster patted her chubby knees and watched Willa with big brown eyes as she dragged the washtub full of sun-warmed water from the porch into the front room. Slipping her arms out of the straps, Willa let the overalls drop to the floor.

Standing in her flour sack drawers and undershirt cut just below her breasts, she studied her reflection in the mirror. Her cheeks were flushed and her eyes were as dull as the river water. "Go see the new doctor," Papa had said. She was sick all right, heartsick, but the new doctor and all his fancy ways couldn't cure it.

She glanced at Aster crawling on the floor. "As long as you stay healthy, baby, we won't be needing him." She picked up the baby and stared into her dark eyes. Then she kissed Aster's rosy cheeks and wrapped her arms around her plump body. She loved her baby dearly in spite of John Sinclair.

"What are we going to do, honey?" she asked, squeezing Aster until she yelled in protest.

Willa sighed. "You're right. What can we do?" Stripping Aster and then herself, Willa sighed as she settled her aching body into the tub of lukewarm water.

Chapter 7
Trapped

Robert Vaughn pulled himself up to a sitting position, tore off his undershirt, and used it to wipe the sweat from the back of his neck.

"That damn dream!" It was the same nightmarish dream he had been having for the past twenty years. Clasping his hands between his knees, he closed his eyes and squeezed them together so hard that tears oozed from the corners. He drew in a deep breath and held it a long time before he blew out with force. From the pounding of his head, he knew that he had consumed too much Jack Daniels, something he had found easy to justify the night before. Staring at the bottle of whiskey, he thought about taking a drink to steady his nerves but decided against it. He heaved himself from the bed and stumbled into the bathroom. Wishing he had a cup of hot coffee, he stripped and climbed into the shower.

It was well after nine o'clock by the time he had finished dressing himself. Reaching for the keys to the doctor's office, he glanced at the rest of the bottle of Jack Daniels that seemed to be calling his name. For the time being at least, he would ignore it.

Word travels fast in a small town, and the news that the newly arrived doctor was single and extremely handsome had spread like a prairie grassfire. All the eligible young ladies devised business right in front of the post office about the time they expected the physician to make his appearance.

A bunch of old men sat on the wooden bench in front of the Gulf Station, not in honor of the new doctor's arrival, but because they were there every day, weather permitting.

Having been at work for several hours, Justin Rider and Tom Henley, the owner of the town's lumberyard, decided to take a break. They turned the corner in front of Raul's Grocery just in time to witness the excitement. The new doctor's custom-built Packard Speedster Runabout came cruising down the street toward his office.

Tom placed his hands in the bib of his overalls. "It looks like the new doc has arrived."

Justin nodded his head. "I'd guess that explains why the gals have turned out in full force."

Tom grinned at Justin. "They all dolled up too, ain't they? Just like it was Saturday."

In unison, the gathered young ladies stopped their chattering as soon as the expensive small car pulled into the parking space marked "Doc."

Robert, who had focused his attention on the sign hanging askew on a small creosote post, was about to open the car door when he realized he was on display. Grimacing, he took a deep breath, self-conscious about the suit of crisp white linen he was wearing. As he emerged from his custom-made Packard, he realized the world he was entering was as foreign to him as it was to his brand-new car.

Robert heard a chorus of giggles from the group of young ladies standing across the street. He ran his eyes over the gathered lot before settling on two girls standing slightly apart from the group, no doubt hoping to be seen a little better by him. So these are the town's giggling and blushing daughters, he thought sarcastically, out husband hunting undoubtedly sent by their mamas to size up the new doctor. The two girls, with their eyes nearly popping out of their heads at the tall, handsome young doctor, whispered behind their hands.

"He's looking at us," Linda Lou gushed. She ran her hand down her new beige, pillowslip dress with the popular wide belt, and then she patted her dark green, autographed, Loretta Young hat.

The girls nudged each other and giggled.

"He's so-oo handsome," one crooned, loud enough to be heard.

A tiny man with a high-pitched voice, who was sitting in a goat-drawn cart, called out, "Howdy, Doc. What kind'a car you got there?"

"It's a Packard," Robert answered, unenthusiastically.

"Ee-uu," Linda Lou gushed, "Who would have dreamed someone like *hi-mm* would actually come to Hornersville?"

Sara Jane stared in wide-eyed admiration for several seconds before she answered her friend. "He doesn't look like any doctor I've ever seen." Secretly Sara Jane thought that she looked like Joan Bennett, especially in the sheer, red dotted cotton batiste dress, with a white organdy hat like Joan had worn in her latest movie.

It was plain to the two men watching from the street corner that the female population was struck by the way providence had smiled on them in the form of an eligible and handsome, young, bachelor doctor.

Justin shook his head. "I've never seen so much fluttering and gushing in my life."

Tom winked. "Disgusting, ain't it?"

Sara Jane lost her composure and said, none too privately, "Oh, those lips! I declare they were made for kissin'."

"Sara Jane!" Linda Lou squealed in mock horror. She leaned close to Sara Jane's ear and whispered from behind her hand, "I would give my eye teeth to take a ride in that car."

The girls sighed as Robert walked to the front door of the office.

"He's got such a cute butt!" Linda Lou said.

It was Sara Jane's turn to admonish. "Sssh," she said with a giggle.

Suddenly, confiding each other's desires came to an abrupt halt as they eyed each other. Instinctively, they knew they would be competing for his attention. There was no doubt in either of their minds that, with a little help from each one's daddy, one of them would succeed. After all, they were the two most popular girls in town, enhanced by their daddy's positions.

Sara Jane's daddy, Mayor Sam Lockwood, a tall, skinny, wormy looking fellow, also owned Lockwood Grocery. He was mighty proud of the niche he had made for himself. Every time his wife Dorothy mentioned moving to Kennett, the county seat, he'd say, "It's better to be a big fish in a little pond."

The Lockwoods attended the First Baptist Church every Sunday where Sam led the choir. Dorothy taught Sunday school and the Girls Auxiliary on Wednesdays. If there ever was a man puffed up with his own importance, it was Sam Lockwood. In his own opinion, he was a right upstanding pillar of the community, and he didn't have time to spend on anyone not equal to his standings.

Bob Vendell, Linda Lou's daddy, owned the local dry goods store. He was a short man with layers of bulging flesh around his middle, a wishy-washy sort, easily manipulated. Like most men of his size, he had a problem keeping his britches pulled up. His constant habit of "hitching" his trousers added to the perception that he was always walking a few steps behind Lockwood in his shadow.

Bud Thomas, owner of the City Café, declared one morning to a group of coffee drinkers that if Lockwood were ever to stop short, old Bob would surely run right up his ass.

Bob and his wife Jackie also attended the First Baptist Church, same as the Lockwoods. Jackie played the piano, while Bob, as head deacon, sat on the front row. Bob Vendell viewed life pretty much the way his friend Sam thought that he should.

Justin Rider eyed the runabout as he walked by it. "I don't think I've ever seen a car like this one. Have you, Tom?"

"Can't say as I have," Tom answered. "What kind do you think it is?"

Justin shrugged his shoulders. He took a few steps into the street. "It says on the back it's a Packard. I think it must be custom-built. She's a beauty, isn't she?"

"She is at that," Tom replied.

Justin shook his head, turned around, and walked backward for several steps, staring at the car. "Do you realize what a custom-built automobile like that must have cost?" He didn't wait for Tom to answer before he added, "Why would a man who can afford to drive a car like this want to practice medicine in a town like Hornersville?"

"I don't know, son," Tom said in his easy way. He maneuvered his toothpick to the other side of his mouth. "If he's half the doctor old Doc Wilson was, we're dang lucky to get him, even for just a little while. All I know is we need not to go lookin' a gift horse in the mouth."

Justin Rider was not satisfied. As far as he was concerned, the new doctor was too fancy—his clothes as well as his car.

The two men walked into the City Café where Bud Thomas was standing by the window with one foot propped on a milk crate, watching the commotion.

"Mornin' men," Bud said as they straddled a couple of stools at the counter. He reached for the coffeepot. "Is the party over?" He poured each man a cup of coffee, set the pot back onto the hot plate, and then placed his elbows on the counter. "So what do you think about him?"

"Justin thinks he's too fancy for us," Tom said as he passed the cream to Justin.

Justin grinned at Bud. "He won't stay here for very long, Bud. I would be willin' to bet money on it."

"I ain't a bettin' man, Justin, but Bonnie will probably be mad at you if you're right." He nodded in the direction of his grinning wife. Bonnie had stuck her head out from the kitchen.

"Just look at her, she's in love with him already,"
Bonnie rolled her eyes. "He shore is pretty, Justin."

Robert Vaughn opened the door to his new office. The screech the door made resounded loudly in the stark room. The wall between the two front rooms had been removed, making one long reception area. A giant pot-bellied stove sat caddy-cornered to one side. A naked light bulb on a length of cord hung from the ceiling. Benches, worn slick over the years, lined the walls beyond the stove. Several butt-sprung rockers for rocking ailing babies were randomly scattered about the room. A massive roll top desk sat in the front near the picture window facing the street.

Shabby as hell, Robert thought, but clean. He walked from the waiting room into an examination room. To his surprise, he found it lined with massive dark Victorian cabinets, the top of each completely covered with apothecary jars of every description. The smell of herbs, roots, and tonics filled the air. A twinge of excitement thrilled him as he examined the huge collection. He didn't have the slightest idea how a country doctor operated, but he knew this apothecary had to be exceptional.

As he was musing on his new life and the strange surroundings, he heard the front door to the office open and then close. The voices of two men bounced from the walls of the empty office. Taking his time, he wiped his hands on his neatly folded linen handkerchief and walked to the front room where a tall, puffed-up skinny fellow greeted him.

"I'm the Mayor," Mr. Skinny said. "Sam Lockwood is my name. This is Bob Vendell," he announced, pointing to his short fat companion.

Mutt and Jeff, Robert thought.

Bob Vendell shook hands with Robert, all the while averting eye contact. He gave his trousers a hitch but said not a word.

"We would like to extend to you the town's welcome," Lockwood continued in a punctilious manner. "Also, the town's apologies for not meeting you when you first arrived. We didn't expect you until today."

"A slight change in plans," Robert lied.

After a brief, perfunctory conversation, the men turned to go. Bob Vendell gestured out the window. "I…I, I like your car," he stammered. "Wh-what kind is it?"

"It's a Packard," Robert answered in a resigned voice. "A damned Packard," he repeated after he'd shut the screen door. He watched the two men cross the street, the short one at least two steps behind the mayor, hitching his trousers every other step as he hurried along on his stubby legs.

Having lost interest, Robert walked idly through the examining room. He opened the door to a room marked "Private" at the very back of the house. It was a small room with a musty smell. At one time, he surmised it had been a refuge for his predecessor. A long table and an over-sized desk and chair crowded the small space. Shelves filled with dusty cardboard boxes lined the remaining two walls. He worked his way around the table to a box and reached inside. It contained two journals. One was filled with what appeared to be carefully printed remedies. From the detailed documentation they were obviously tried and tested over the years by Wilson. The second journal was marked "The Holler."

Robert moved the clutter around so he could seat himself at the desk. After plugging in an ancient electric fan, he leaned back in the chair, propped up his feet, and opened the journal entitled The Holler. The remedies could wait for another time.

Expecting a dreary country doctor's bleak musings on disease and death, Robert Vaughn was surprised to stumble on information about a seemingly closed, isolated society of uneducated, mostly half-breeds who survived by bootlegging, picking cotton, and fishing. But most interesting to him were the details of a very beautiful woman named Willa Sinclair.

An hour later, he was brought back to reality by the rumbling of his stomach. The food in his refrigerator, which had not made much of an impression the night before, suddenly seemed welcoming.

Chapter 8
Half-Blood

Justin Rider, one-half Indian, was well acquainted with the term, "Wah-who" which some folks liked to call those of Native American descent. But he didn't give a damn what they called him because he was proud of his ancestry. As far as Justin was concerned, better men had never lived than his father and grandfather, both full-blooded Osage.

Like Ben Melton, they had spent their lives in the great swamps along Little River. His daddy, Jim, was a jack-of-all-trades. His grandfather, Will Sky, had worked as a gunsmith and a blacksmith, a lucrative business for as long as the commercial hunting and fishing flourished.

Justin also had a passion for hunting and fishing. He had learned at the knee of the master, Will Sky. It was a sad day in the old Indian's life when the engineering wonder, as they called it, drained the swamps. One day, he walked down to the riverbank, turned his face to the east, the place of mystery, sang his last prayer, and gave up his spirit. Justin built a special little retreat that he dubbed "the Sky House" on the very spot where Will Sky had expired.

When Justin was sixteen, his daddy also passed away. That changed his direction in life. Someone had to take care of his mama. It was a hard decision for him to make, but he dropped out of school and walked the streets of Hornersville literally begging for a job. No one would even consider hiring a kid, let alone a half-Indian kid, no one, that is, except Tom Henley. Tom was a gangly man with a heart as big as his body. He always contended that he never regretted showing compassion for the lanky kid from the Holler. In fact, he loved the boy like the son he never had. When he spoke of Justin, his homely face would break into a big smile. His favorite story recounted the day he gave Justin the job of cleaning up after the work crew.

"Right quick, I sensed his keenness. I'd watched him work and saw how quickly he learned the trade of carpentry. Why, in no time at all he was my helper. In three years time, I taught him all I knew." The conversation would always end with Tom giving a hearty laugh. "Now he's better'n me."

Justin was on his way home from work and thinking of Ruby.

Ruby, Ruby, luscious Ruby, with long, thick, honey-gold hair and laughing sapphire-colored eyes. She was a sight to behold in the Holler, and no one knew it any better than Justin "Jay Sky" Rider. Long before he reached the fork in the road, Justin knew he was going to take the footpath down Perry Hill. He told himself that he wanted to find out if Ruby would go to the dance on Saturday night. But what he really hoped for was that Ruby would meet him later in the evening in their favorite spot.

Justin descended Perry Hill in long easy strides. He rounded the corner in seconds, cramming his work cap into his back pocket before mounting the steps of the dilapidated front porch. In one quick motion, he bounded to the door and knocked.

Maw NanEmmer answered the door. Seeing that it was Justin, she removed the "dip and chew" willow stick from the corner of her snuff-stained mouth, just long enough to give him a near-toothless smile. She replaced the stick and laced her fingers together over her stomach. She liked this boy. Every time she saw him, she considered him a treat to an old woman's eyes.

Nannie Emma Wilkerson was at least seventy years old, if she was a day. She had a long wrinkled face that looked as if it had been dipped in a mud hole. Her sparse white hair, which she combed once a week with a fine- tooth comb, was twisted into a bun on the top of her head. She had been a tall woman in her prime, but over the years she developed a huge hump on her back due to brittle bones. Nannie Emma's people, along with Lester and Chester Higgers, better known as Big Boy and Little Son, were migrant mountaineers from the Appalachian Highlands.

Maw wore an ankle length black skirt and dingy white blouses in the same style she had worn for the last thirty years. She also practiced the spraddled stance of the backwoods woman; the exception being Maw never felt the need for privacy. She peed anytime and anywhere she felt like it. Then she'd use her petticoat to dry herself and resume whatever it was she was doing. Maw changed her clothes every two weeks. Due to her habits, by the time the second week rolled around, the pungent smell of urine enveloped her like a fog.

"Hi, Maw, how ya doin'?" Justin inquired when she opened the door.

"Doin ta'ble, son, except the rheumatism has come back on me. Ruby ain't here. Ya wanna come in and wait on'er?" she asked with a grin and a twinkle in her faded and watery blue eyes.

Justin watched as a stream of snuff dribbled down her chin and joined several other dribbles on her blouse. "Can't, Maw. If you will, please tell Ruby for me that I stopped by to see if she might like to go to the dance on Saturday."

Justin left Maw standing on the porch. He had a grin on his face. He was confident that Ruby would not only get the message, but that she would understand it.

Later that afternoon the twins helped Justin hoist his boat out of the water and up to the bank where Ben Melton waited.

"Have you seen the new doctor yet, boy?" Little Son asked as they lifted the boat onto the crude saw horses.

Justin scoffed, then nodded his head. "He's the main topic of conversation around town these days."

Little Son grinned and threw a few chunks of pitch into the iron pot hanging over the fire. Ben grabbed the paddle and stirred until the pitch melted. When the tar was ready for Justin to use, Little Son puffed his way over to the hand pump under the shade tree and pumped himself a fruit jar of cool water. After shooing two old hens from the wooden bench, he sat down and stretched out his stubby legs. He wiped his face with a bandanna handkerchief, then took his finger and dug what was left of the tobacco from his cheek. He rinsed his mouth, then took a long swig of water. Feeling satisfied and refreshed, he reached into his pocket for a fresh chaw.

"Old John said he's quite a city dude, fancy as all hell," he said, just before poking his jaw full of fresh tobacco.

Ben gave a snort of contempt. "I reckoned John and Rabbit didn't miss a thing since they had a ringside seat from the jail house window."

Ben rubbed his balding head with his handkerchief and dropped down on the bench alongside of Little Son. He slapped the front pockets of his overalls for the makings of a cigarette. "We'll never have another one like old Doc Wilson. Damned if I know what we'll do in case of bad sickness." He was thinking of Willa.

"I feel sure you can count this one out," Justin said. "I doubt seriously he'll hang around long enough to unpack. As Miz Effie would say, being the observant woman that she is, he's a fish out of water."

Surprised that Jay Sky of all people would be negative about the new doctor, Little Son blinked several times before he asked, "Whut makes you say that?"

Normally, Justin avoided talking over the twin's head but, for the moment, he forgot his tongue. "From his appearance and manner, not to mention the car he drives, I'd say that he was born with the proverbial silver spoon in his mouth. He's lived the life of the cre'me de la cre'me of St. Louis society. I'd bet on it. It just doesn't make any sense, him being down here."

"I don't know much about this creamy deli cream stuff," Little Son grunted.

Big Boy, who up to this point had been silent, spoke up. "I think I can cut right to the chase," he said. "Whut yore tryin' to tell us is that he's the kind that thinks *his* shit don't stink."

Justin grinned. "I reckon," he said.

"Well now..." Little Son drawled.

The other three observed him grinning like a Cheshire cat. They looked at each other and exchanged a conspiratorial smile as if to say, here it comes.

Little Son's eyes began to dance. He took his time chewing and spitting a stream of tobacco juice toward the water. "The way I see it, boys, beans or steak, it don't matter what a feller is use to eatin'. In the end it all turns to shit. Irregardless of what highfalutin folks think about themselves, all shit smells the same, don't it?"

Bean, the one and only Holler dog, could be heard barking in the distance. All three men turned to see him racing across the Holler in a loping, floppy-eared gait. He jumped on Little Son's chest, nearly knocking him to the ground.

"Whoa, Hoss!" Little Son grunted. He laughed affectionately as he rubbed the dog's head.

The men knew that simple-minded Pebo would not be far behind. The man-child Peter Boyd had never had a home. He didn't even know he had a father until, at the age of fourteen, the state owned orphanage where he had lived since infancy told him he would be going to live with his father. But as soon as the authorities left the Holler, Albert Boyd packed his new family and took off down the river, leaving retarded Pebo behind to fend for himself.

Pebo nodded a howdy to Ben and the twins. "How's yore mama doin'?" he inquired.

The men nodded and said automatically, "Doin' fine, Pebo."

Pebo went directly to where Jay Sky was standing. "I got a note fer ye from Miz Rube." He rummaged into his pockets, then looked at Justin in dismay. Justin reached over, felt under the collar of Pebo's shirt, and unpinned the note.

"I ferget, best buddy."

"I know," Justin said gently. "It's okay, Pebo."

Justin stuck the note in his pocket without reading it.

"You ain't gonna read it to us?" Big Boy teased.

"Nope," Justin said and headed for the cottonwood tree for a little privacy.

Pebo dropped down by the edge of the water to wait. He considered Jay Sky to be his best friend in all the world. He liked the twins and Ben, too. They were all good to him. Fed him and everything. But it was Jay Sky that he loved best of all. Jay Sky spent long hours with him, teaching him all the stuff he needed to know, such as taking baths in the river and saying things like "please" and "thank you." Now he even knew how to be polite and ask about folks' mamas. Jay Sky let him sleep in the Sky House down on the river where he never let anyone go not even Miz Rube. Jay Sky said it was his own private space, but he would share it with him. But he must promise never to let anyone go inside. Faithful Pebo would literally have died defending the honor.

Alone under the cottonwood, Justin opened the note. Ruby wanted him to meet her that evening. He quickly scribbled his reply, called Pebo, and pinned it under his collar, then sent him back to Ruby's.

Ruby Wilkerson was the first woman Justin had ever known in the biblical sense. Actually the only one, but he would never admit to it. Ruby, a master of the art, so to speak, had taught him all he knew. He, like most young men of his age, was an ardent student, willing to work overtime if necessary to do his instructor proud.

Ruby sat under the oak tree in front of Maw NanEmmer's shack waiting for Pebo to return. Fresh from the beauty shop, she had her honey-colored hair piled on top of her head in tiny ringlets. Her professionally painted nails and long slim legs, oiled to a shine, glistened in the sunlight that danced through the foliage of the giant oak tree. Dainty feet, encased in white sandals, sported bright red toenails that matched her fingernails, full red lips, and polka dot sundress.

The secret affair that Ruby was having with the businessman in Kennett, although it wasn't really a secret, afforded her luxuries no other woman in the Holler could afford. It plainly served as a bone of contention among most of the other females.

"There she is all decked out in her beauty shop do, just waitin' to be picked up," they'd whisper to each other in passing. Only respect for Maw NanEmmer kept them halfway civil to the spirited young woman, whom they secretly envied.

Ruby was a kept woman, and no one knew it any better than she. In essence, they could say Ruby did what she had to do, rather like Justin did when he was forced to quit school and take care of his mother. But no one viewed Ruby so kindly, except Justin Rider and his good friend, Willa Sinclair.

Ruby watched until she saw Pebo lumbering up the path with the ever faithful Bean trotting at his heels.

"I done whut you said, Miz Rube. You bet'che I did."

"Miz Rube thanks you, Pebo." She smiled and reached under his collar. Then she pressed a nickel into his hand.

Pebo headed for Mays' grocery. Realizing he had forgotten his manners, he turned and walked back to where Ruby sat reading the note.

"Miz Rube?"

Ruby smiled. "Yes, Pebo?" she said gently.

"Please to thank you and how's yore mama doin'?"

Later in the evening, Ruby Wilkerson met Jay Sky in their special place not far from the Sky house.

"Hi, handsome," she said with eyes glowing in anticipation.

"Hello, beautiful," he said lazily. With a heart-breaking grin on his sculptured face, Jay Sky leaned down with a welcoming kiss. Ruby opened her mouth to him and his tongue touched hers. After several long deep kisses, Ruby found what she was looking for. She lifted her dress and straddled his lap. Closing her eyes, she rocked back and forth, giving and taking pleasure. Much later, she lay beside Jay Sky stroking his long lean body ever so lightly. She raised herself to her elbow and gazed at him through wistful eyes. Lovingly, she ran her fingers through his hair. Hair as dark as the Holler night.

Chapter 9
With Ill Will

For the next few weeks the ladies of the town, in true southern fashion, fattened Robert and fawned over him, at least as much as he would allow. Young ladies of every description kept the street hot, delivering pies, cakes, and homemade cookies. Above all they let him know with dress, perfume, and sidelong glances that they were available.

Leading the pack was none other than Sara Jane Lockwood. To Robert, Sara Jane was different. In her eyes he read an unmistakable message. He must be careful with this one, he told himself. She could be dangerous. He did not intend to dally carelessly with her and get stuck in this hick town. Though he avoided her as best he could, it would have been easier to avoid the mosquitoes along the river. When he got the urge to take her up on the unspoken promise in her eyes, he would think of Wilson's journals and of an unfortunate beauty by the name of Willa Sinclair.

By this time, another woman had entered Robert Vaughn's life, a most unlikely lady. Entering the office that first day, he found a tiny woman sitting at the huge desk by the window. Fully dressed in white, she never moved a muscle for several long moments, giving him the impression that she had been dipped in starch, ironed and placed into position.

When she finally looked up, her face was completely devoid of any expression whatsoever.

"Good morning, Doctor Vaughn," she stated.

"Uh, good morning..." He didn't have the least idea who she was, that is until he saw the nametag pinned on her chest, "Miss Hodges?"

"Miss Birdie will do, please," she informed him in her crisp, efficient voice. Robert deemed the name most applicable. Miss Birdie was a small woman with a tiny head and beady eyes. Her manner was quick and flitty in every way.

"Your first patient is in five minutes. I suggest you hurry."

Once he was safely out of earshot, he turned and gave her a second look. "Well, the hell you say, Old Bird!" He muttered to her back, "Who hired you, anyway?"

Birdie Hodges had not waited to be hired. The job of being the doctor's nurse was hers and hers alone as far as she was concerned, and no one else in town would dare apply for it.

Robert suddenly remembered a nurse named Hodges in Wilson's journals. "Well, I'll be damned!" Though he didn't really like her, the old Bird soon became the glue that held him together. Under the guidance of Birdie Hodges, the practice flourished. But Robert did not. Robert Vaughn had been lonely for most of his life; one might say a loneliness of the spirit.

To counteract, he had spent a great deal of time indulging in physical pleasures with the opposite sex. In his present hell-on-earth, to compensate for his lack of physical contact, he now drank to excess each night while reading Wilson's intriguing journal. He especially enjoyed Wilson's account of the Higger twins, whom he referred to as a pair of piss-poor bootleggers.

Recognizing how bored he was, how humdrum life was in Hornersville, Robert Vaughn, well into his evening cup of escape, devised a plan to do some bootlegging. Even after he'd sobered up, the idea seemed solid, downright challenging in fact. As a first step, he decided to take the marshal up on his invitation to tour the territory.

Cushman stopped the car. "I reckon by now you've heard of the Holler. At the foot of this here hill is a path that leads to it."

"Shall we take a look?" To Robert's dismay, Cushman shook his head no.

"Ain't nothing down there but a bunch of squat-who's and wah-who's. I don't reckon you be wantin' to see it, that is less'n you're interested in buying a little moonshine from the bootleggers. Besides, there ain't no road leadin' down there." Cushman turned and spat a long stream of tobacco juice out of the car window into the dust.

Feigning surprise, Robert declared, "Bootleggers?"

"Yeah, twins they are, by the name of Higgers. We've tried for years to catch'em at it. We got as much chance as a fart in a whirlwind." He eyed Robert to see how he was taking it. Noting that the doctor's interest had heightened, he added, "It makes my job a little tedious some times. You see there ain't many ways to get into this Holler. There's this here footpath you see going down the hill. That there dirt road over yonder will git'che a little closer. No matter which way you go, you still gotta walk," he said as if walking was a form of torture. "Of course, you can boat down the river, if you've a mind to." He peered at Robert. Hoping to impress the city slicker a little more, he added, "Back in '27, we raided a shine-still a mile north of Coon Island on Little River, between Caruth and Cotton Plant. Took'em by surprise, we did."

"No kidding?" Robert exclaimed.

"Yep, we shore did. I reckon if I set my mind to it, I could figure out a way to outsmart them twins. I'd bet you a dime to a hole in a donut, they know by now that we're sittin' up here talkin' about 'em." He looked all around the car. "By tomorrow, they can probably tell you whut we been sayin'."

Robert grunted and with a few words of encouragement urged him on. "Tell me about the people living down there."

"Well," he said. "It ain't nothing to be proud of. But there's a lot of folks there and has been ever since they got rid of the swamps. Old Doc Wilson use'to go down there all the time. Probably what killed him. Nobody messes with them much as long as they don't kill anybody with bad whiskey."

"Is the Holler in the city limits?"

"Naw, they all just a bunch of squatters, squat-who's or, if some Injun's blood is mixed in, wah-who's. They live in tents and shacks," he said with a flourish of his arm. "Why, right around this hill is an old man living in a car. Damnedest sight you ever did see."

Robert was not interested in any old man. He wanted to know who owned the Holler. "If these people don't own the property they live on, then who does?"

"I don't reckon anybody owns it anymore. Taxes ain't been paid on it in years. Can't say as anybody wants it. It ain't good for nothing but flooding." The marshal paused for a moment and scratched his protruding stomach. "Seems like I remember hearing that the last feller what owned it, which was many a year ago, was a bootlegger, too."

Robert had all the information he needed. The very next day, he made a trip to Kennett, the county seat where he bought the Holler for back taxes. No one would ever know he owned it unless it became necessary. Owning the Holler was a little security for what he had in mind. His ace in the hole, he called it.

Chapter 10
To Have Title

Robert rounded a curve on the dirt road which by-passed the Holler. Slowing the Packard to a near crawl, he gazed longingly at the path that lazily meandered into the tall cottonwood trees, then disappeared from sight. Intuition told him that his aspirations were foolish. Nevertheless, he parked the Packard and climbed out. Since it was a bitterly cold day, no one was in sight. Ignoring the well-worn path, he trudged deliberately through tall dried grass and brush to skirt the edge of the holler and view it undetected. As he plunged deeper, the grass turned into a weedy thicket and Robert noticed that his clothing was completely covered with the sticky seeds of beggars' lice. Inescapably neat by nature, he crouched down to pick his pants' legs clean, and in doing so, felt a gust of wind drive dust and debris into his face.

"Damn!" he exclaimed, as he lost his balance and stumbled. By the time he recovered, he was astounded to find that the tiny clearing known as Happy Holler was only a few yards ahead of him. In amazement, his eyes panned the box-like shacks; each mounted on shoulder-high stilts, made either of cypress logs or abandoned crossties from the railroad. Stovepipes protruded from every available space. He watched as the wood smoke barely cleared the pipes before the breath of the freezing wind blew it horizontally, before forcing the suffocating smoke down around the shacks. For a brief second, the shacks seemed to be floating in the settling noxious clouds of haze.

He shook his head, blinked his eyes, and reluctantly turned to go. Blocking his exit was a strange-looking giant of a man. Robert, unaccustomed to unsettling happenings, attempted to assess the situation. He could try passing the obstacle or go the other way. Reckoning the size of the obstacle, he headed in the direction of the river.

The Higger twins, along with Ben Melton, who had been alerted early by a birdcall from Pebo, dropped what they were doing and assembled on the ditch dump to watch the uninvited intruder.

Robert, walking as quickly as possible, kept a wary eye on the long shadow of the giant following him. As he passed by the shacks on the edge of the Holler, he had an eerie feeling that he was being watched by multiple sets of eyes. He couldn't help but jump when a dog's barking pierced the silence. Whirling about to defend himself, he noticed that the giant was gaining on him. With each cautious step he took, the dog's barking grew louder. Robert was no coward, but he was out of his element, and he knew it. He cursed himself for being so nosy.

The dog had positioned himself between Robert and a shack that sat on the bank of the river. He could do little now but stand still and hold his ground.

The three men who had been observing him from the ditch-dump approached him quickly when they saw the standoff between the barking hellhound and the visitor.

"Hesh, Bean!" Little Son said softly.

The dog stopped his infernal barking and lay down. Despite the cold, the stalking giant dropped into the dirt beside Bean.

Noticing that Robert's eyes were still darting back and forth between the giant man-child and the dog, Ben Melton volunteered, "This here's Pebo."

Pebo, grinning from ear to ear, bobbed his head. "Please to thank you. How's yore mama doin'?"

"This here feller doin' the greeting is Old String Bean," Little Son said, pointing to the dog. "You can call him Bean." As he spoke, Little Son glanced at Ben, whose eyes, as usual, were twinkling with humor.

Robert gave a slight nod in the direction of Pebo and Bean. He turned back to the men. Clearing his throat, he announced, "My name is Robert Vaughn. I'm the new physician in town. Maybe you've heard of me."

"Little Son Higgers here. This here's Ben Melton, and that'n lookin' jest like me's my brother, Big Boy."

Looks of suspicion passed between the twins and Ben Melton.

"Whut's brung you to the Holler, Doc? Ain't nobody sick down here that I knowed about, is'er Ben?"

"I don't reckon there is," Ben answered, pulling his coat collar up around his ears and then thrusting both hands deep into the pockets of the old wool mackinaw.

Little Son squatted on his heels and settled himself against the large cottonwood tree that stood in front of his home. He took a plug of tobacco from his pocket, cut himself a chaw with his knife, and poked it in his jaw. Big Boy did the same.

"Tabbaccy?" they said in unison. Once again their eyes glistened with humor.

"No, no thank you." Robert stammered. The chewing tobacco made him think of the marshal. Robert Vaughn hated tobacco.

When no one said a word, Robert realized the men were waiting for him to tell them what he was doing in the Holler. He searched his mind for a reason. "I'm afraid I'm a little lost," he lied. "I was trying to take a look at the river."

"Well, there she is, Doc." Big Boy nodded in the direction of the water.

"Sorta cold to be lookin' at'er today," Little Son put in, then spit a stream of tobacco juice at Robert's feet.

"Today's the kind'a day when a feller gets out, does what he's gotta do, then high tails'er back in the house," Big Boy added, pointing toward the outhouse.

Ben lowered his head and adjusted his hat to hide the grin on his face.

"I see what you mean," Robert said with a shiver. He was not properly dressed for the weather. He found himself in a sticky situation. Clearly they were questioning his sanity, as well as his reason for being in the Holler. No doubt they would laugh at him if they really knew his mission. He would have to wait, do what he wanted to do, but all in good time.

Little Son pushed himself from the base of the tree and stood upright. He could see the doctor was uncomfortable. Though Little Son Higgers was not an educated man, he was a very shrewd one. He knew Robert was in the Holler for a purpose. There were too many ways to get to the river without coming through the Holler, and the doctor had been in Hornersville long enough to know that.

Purposefully, Little Son waited for the doctor to make the next move. He's got something in his craw. Wonder why he don't just spit it out, he thought, as he spat a stream of tobacco juice, this time aiming at a dirt clod. Hitting his target, he shifted his gaze back to Robert and waited.

Since he couldn't think of a thing more to say, Robert decided it was time to end his visit. "It's nice meeting you gentlemen," he said, extending his hand.

"You, too, Doc. See-ya-aroun,'" Big Boy answered.

"Tak-id-eezy now," Little Son added.

Ben tipped his hat.

Robert turned to go. Since it was Pebo's duty to see that any strangers who accidentally found their way into the Holler also found their way out, he fell in behind him.

"What the hell do you think that was all about, Ben?" Big Boy asked as he and Ben headed for home.

"Who knows, maybe he was lost?" Ben answered. "But I kinda doubt it."

After Pebo and Bean had seen Robert safely to his car, Bean raced back to the Holler ahead of Pebo. When he reached Little Son, waiting for Pebo to return to the Holler, he wagged his tail and licked his hand.

"You done a good job, Bean. You and old Pebo wouldn't hurt a flea, but 'che sure 'nuff put the scare in that doc." Little Son scratched the dog's ears with both hands. "You the best damn dog in the Holler, I'm here to tell ya. Course you the only damn dog in the Holler. But if you ain't smart enough to figure that out fer yoreself, I shore ain't gonna be the one to tell ya." Little Son pondered for a few seconds. "Wonder whut he wanted, Bean?"

Bean whined, wagged, and licked at Little Son's face. "You don't know, huh, boy?" Little Son could see Pebo in the distance hurrying back for his penny. He bent down and gently slapped the dog's sides. "Me neither, Bean, me neither," he said. "But I'm damn shore of one thing, partner, he weren't lost. He had to have come through the thicket to have all 'em stickers hanging from his butt."

Willa Sinclair had also heard Bean's bark. She hadn't bothered to hurry to the window as the rest of the Holler did. Aster had been fretting all morning. Effie said she might be trying to cut teeth, but Willa wasn't so sure. By the time she placed the ailing baby on the bed and covered her from the cold, the stranger had already passed. She barely took time to glance out the back window. Feeling certain that she was going to be in for a long night with the baby, Willa turned her back on the noise outside, raised the covers, and climbed into the bed beside her baby, unaware that what destiny had in store for her was standing not more than a few feet away. As she drifted off to sleep, she wondered what was going to happen to her and her child.

Chapter 11
In Desperation

"Hush little baby don't you cry. Mama's gonna buy you a…" Willa paused in her song to whisper to herself, "Mama can't buy you anything." Tears of desperation came to her eyes. She reached for a soft piece of cloth, soaked it in cool water, leaned forward, and bathed her baby's head against the fever. As she did, Aster's body shook violently from coughing.

Outside, the number three wash tub, which hung on the side of the tiny two-roomed shack, thumped in regular rhythm with the cold north wind. The spasms of coughing and gasping of thirteen-month old Aster, mixed with the howling wind, intensified Willa's feeling of hopelessness. Tired and aching from being up most of the night, Willa crept to the wooden bench beside the kitchen table and sat. She rested her head on her arms. How easy it would be to sleep. Instead, she pulled herself to her feet, walked to the opening between the kitchen and the front room, and pulled aside the raggedy quilt, which served as a door.

As she approached the bed in the corner of the front room, she gave it a kick with her foot. "Wake up, John, and listen to me. Aster has a fever this morning." Willa watched him only long enough to see his habitual uncaring expression appear as he rolled over and then without a word, closed his eyes.

Not expecting any further response, Willa returned to the kitchen. She had to prepare breakfast. Swallowing the lump in her throat, she tried not to notice the weevils she sifted from the flour.

John Sinclair sat up on the side of the bed. His scruffy hair was a tousled mess. His long johns reeked of sweat and urine. Stirring the pile of dirty clothing on the floor with his foot, he dug out a soiled pair of pants and rummaged in the pockets for a cigarette. When he could find nothing to smoke, he scowled and ran his tongue over his coated teeth. He searched the room with his eyes, hoping for a cigarette butt to get rid of the bad taste in his mouth. In Willa's house, he knew, he would never find one. This only added to his infuriation. He retaliated by giving the clean clothing at the foot of his bed a vengeful shove to the floor.

"She thinks I'm gonna put'em on, but the hell I am!" he muttered and pulled on his dirty pants, trampling the clean ones in the process.

Through the paper-thin walls, Willa listened and wondered how she could have ever let this happen to her.

"Why don't you kick him out, Willa?" Papa kept asking her. She had no ready answer.

John eventually stumbled into the kitchen. Willa's eyes followed him to the dry sink. She noted the small broken blood vessels forming tell-tale patches on his cheeks and nostrils.

Snatching the wash pan from the wall, John poured a dipper of cold water over his head.

"John, Aster coughed and choked all night," Willa told him. She kept her voice low so that she wouldn't disturb the baby.

John gave a grunt and turned his back. "You don't need to tell me about no damn coughing," he grumbled. "I ain't deaf. I couldn't sleep at all for that damn noise." He dipped his hands into the wash pan and rubbed his tangled hair and unshaven face with the cold water.

Fumbling until he found the clean towel, he scrubbed his face with it, leaving fuzz stuck haphazardly about on his week old stubble.

Noting the fuzz and the dirty brown streaks on the towel, Willa sighed and turned her back so that she wouldn't have to look at him. She finished frying the fatback. Then she removed the hot biscuits from the tiny tin oven. "I think you've heard about the new doctor," she commented. She added some flour to the hot grease and let it brown until it turned nearly black in color. Effie had taught her that lacking milk for the gravy, this method would provide a little flavor. She added the water as quickly as possible and continued to stir the mixture until it thickened properly.

"I've heard he was in the Holler yesterday. I wonder if he'll see Aster."

"Well, if he was here, why didn't you just run right out and ask him in?" John sneered. "You know damn well he'll see her *if* you've got the damn money to pay him for it."

"I don't have any money left, John. You should know—since you stole the last I had. I know better than to expect you to give me any."

Willa sat down at the kitchen table to eat her breakfast. She tried not to think of the weevils. When she finished, she lifted a small dishpan from its hook on the wall over the dry sink. Automatically, she held it up to the light to check it for any more holes. There were four "mend-its" in the bottom already. Filling the pan from the teakettle on the oil stove, she added some of Effie's homemade soap and washed the dishes.

John looked at his breakfast; his stomach was feeling queasy. He sniffed at the pungent smell of the last of the fatback. His upper lip curling in distaste, he pushed it back. He gave Willa a go-to-hell look. As far as he was concerned, she was the reason he was feeling sick. Noisily, he tromped to the front room, grabbed up his nasty old jacket, and rummaged in his pockets to see if he still had his money. He wanted to get the hell out of the house before she found out about it. Turning his back, he counted it. He had almost two dollars. It was enough money for him to get damn good and drunk on. He stomped back through the kitchen and out the back door, letting the door slam with a bang. "Serves her right if the baby wakes up," he said and stalked off toward the river. The very thought of the whiskey caused him to lick his lips. He knew the Higgers wouldn't sell him any, but all he had to do was go find Rabbit.

Aster stirred. Willa held her breath until the baby settled back down. She carefully greased the iron skillet and hung it in its place on the wall over the oil stove, fully aware that she wouldn't be using it for frying any more meat for quite a while. Willa finished cleaning the kitchen. Wrinkling her nose at the smell of the front room, she grabbed John's bedding in the same manner she did every morning, carried it to the backyard, and threw it over the clothesline. She hurried back into the house to drag John's straw mattress to the porch where she threw it over the wood box to air out.

Aster suffered through another spasm of coughing. "Don't you worry, honey, Mama is going to get you a doctor one way or other." She stroked Aster's head. For herself, she would never beg for anything. But for her baby, she would do most anything. She looked out of the window. It was a good mile or more to town. She had walked it before carrying Aster. She knew she could do it again.

Chapter 12
Fate

Willa stepped out of the cold wind into the sheltered area between the Merchants and Planters Bank and Gossett's Cleaners. After checking the baby, she readjusted Aster's weight to relieve her aching arms, squared her shoulders, and headed across the street toward the doctor's office.

At the precise moment that Willa was crossing the street, Robert Vaughn opened his south-facing window and drew in a cleansing breath. He saw someone moving briskly across the street, hunched against the wind, her face hidden by the posture she assumed in an attempt to keep her bundle warm. He closed his eyes and grumbled, "Another damn patient."

Willa climbed the steps and opened the door. A strong gust jerked the knob out of her hand, causing the door to swing open and crash against the wall with a bang.

Miss Birdie, looking like a snowbird presiding over a drab and dreary flock, gave her a reproving stare.

"Sorry," Willa muttered. She looked around until she found a small vacant spot to squeeze into behind the pot-bellied stove, receiving sour looks from the waiting patients. "Sorry," she said again as she sat down.

Propping Aster up against her shoulder, she took a deep breath, lay her head back, and rested it against the wall.

Robert, having filled his lungs to full capacity with clean, frosty air, shut the window. The endless flow of bedraggled humanity that kept coming through the doors had overwhelmed him completely. He cast one last yearning gaze down the deserted street and out across the railroad tracks toward freedom. He knew he must continue to call in the patients before the Old Bird flew in to see what he was doing. Gritting his teeth, he willed himself the strength to finish the day.

Willa Sinclair waited and watched as Miss Birdie, peering over horn-rimmed glasses perched on the end of her nose, called each patient's name. One by one the room emptied until she finally announced in her starchiest voice to the all but empty room, "Willa Sinclair, the doctor will see you now."

Rubbing his neck and flexing his aching shoulders, Robert stepped to the sink on the back wall to wash his hands. Behind him, he heard the door open and close then a slight hesitation before someone crossed the room. Since he had absolutely no interest in the patient's identity, he kept his back turned. At length, he reached for the towel and dried each finger carefully, deliberately as if deriving some small pleasure by delaying the inevitable just a little longer. His lip curled in disgust as he caught a glimpse of his reflection in the mirror. He sighed, gave the towel a toss in the direction of the laundry hamper, turned, and his eyes narrowed in disbelief. After all this time, there she was, standing in front of him in bedraggled dignity, wearing a threadbare coat and an exhausted mushroom of a hat.

He picked up the file that the Old Bird had left him. It was indeed the elusive Willa Sinclair.

"My name is Willa Sinclair," she told him in a husky voice, a result of having breathed the extremely cold air.

Robert's eyes scanned her with the intensity of the predator. Even wrapped in the sad old coat, he could see Dr. Wilson had not exaggerated. She was everything he had anticipated, more, in fact. From the glorious head of hair protruding from the disgrace called a hat, down to the dark lashes shadowing her lovely face.

Putting her best foot forward, Willa stated, "At the moment, I can't pay you money to see my baby, but I am not here asking you for charity. If you'll treat her, I'm more than willing to work for you to pay the bill." She glanced around the office. "I can clean for you..." Her voice trailed off, and an awkward silence fell over the room.

Robert gave himself a mental shake. Fate has played into his hands when he least expected it, and he was acting like a dunce.

"We won't worry about that just now," he said quickly. "Place the baby on the table and stand beside her, please." Willa crossed in front of him, so close he could smell the scent of clean air that she brought with her.

"Her name is Aster," Willa offered.

"Hello, Aster. Glad to meet you." Robert laughed and rubbed the baby's head.

The baby's wheezing, the frequency of her pulse, plus the difficulty in breathing told him she had a bad case of the croup.

Several times during the examination, Willa felt his eyes brush over her. Certain that he was being critical of her appearance, she felt a stab of defiance. Lifting her chin, she squared her shoulders and let her eyes sweep over him. What gives you the right to judge me? Raising her chin still higher, she thought, what do I care as long as you make Aster well?

The doctor's professional distance finally unnerved her and caused her to forget her defiance. She blurted out, "How is she? Do you think she's going to be all right?"

Pausing before answering as if he must be careful with his words, he replied, "I would expect so. All she needs is a little medicine."

Aster grabbed the silk tie dangling in front of her and brought it to her mouth. With some effort, the doctor retrieved his tie and then placed the baby in her mother's arms.

Directing Willa into the small inner office, he moved the chair by the side of his desk slightly forward and motioned for her to be seated.

Despite her attitude of defiance, Willa was uncomfortable, more so than she had ever been in her life. Perching herself on the edge of the chair, she clutched Aster to her breast.

Robert, who was biding his time by making a few medical notes, finished and swiveled his chair around to face her. In the process, his knees brushed hers.

"You're from the Holler," he stated.

"Yes," she answered. Feeling defensive, she added, "Is there a problem with that?"

"Not at all," he said, giving her one of his rare and dazzling smiles. "I was down there only yesterday."

A muscle twitched at the corner of Willa's mouth. Papa had told her about the twins giving him a hard time.

Aster gurgled, twisted her body, and smiled at Robert. He returned the smile and leaned forward. It seemed to Willa that his mouth was but inches away from her mouth, when he suddenly lowered his head to the baby and kissed its crown, leaving the spicy scent of his hair in her nostrils.

"So you're willing to work to pay for my services?" he asked her in the most cultivated voice she had ever heard. "If you're serious, it can be arranged."

Moments later, Robert stood at the window and watched her disappear in the direction of the Holler. "Yes!" he shouted. She was far more than he had anticipated. "I believe you are going to serve my needs very well, Willa Sinclair, very well."

As the second cog in his wheel of diversion disappeared from sight, Robert's life was a lot brighter. Now, in fact, he knew exactly how he was going to get into the Holler. He would wait, and this time he would be much better prepared when he entered the private domain of the Higger twins.

Three days later, Willa responded to a knock on the door of the tiny shack. She stood frozen to the spot, staring at the apparition before her.

There stood Dr. Vaughn in a cashmere jacket and white linen shirt, leaning against the doorjamb and smiling as casually as possible.

"Hello," he stated and waited for an invitation to come in. When he didn't receive it, he shifted uneasily and finally asked, "Do you mind if I come in?"

"John's not at home," she stammered. She closed her eyes at her own stupidity.

"I didn't come to see John. I am here to check on Aster, Mrs. Sinclair."

"Oh," she said, flushing with embarrassment. She stepped back and let him enter. Patting her burning cheeks, she followed him to the center of the room. Her eyes were on his head. She couldn't help but notice how perfectly his hair grew to a point at the nape of his neck. Hair, she thought, my own must be a mess. Her hands darted to her head, then down the sides of the faded dungarees and oversized flannel shirt that covered her body. Unconsciously, she gave the tail of the shirt a vicious tug.

At that moment, the tiny room claimed Robert's attention, the likes of which he had never seen before in his affluent life. A diminutive bed, hardly large enough for one person, sat neatly made against the long wall. A homemade storage box, holding an oil lamp and what appeared to be a basket of mending, flanked it. A rag-tag dresser hosting an odd assortment of things, a well-worn oak rocker with cushions made largely of worn out denim, and a wood-burning stove with a pot of beans simmering on the top completed the room.

Slowly his eyes traveled from the furnishings to the flour sack curtains, simply embroidered, starched and ironed, and then to the spotlessly clean though water-warped floor. It was covered with unmatching, rag-tag scraps of linoleum, topped here and there with colorful rag rugs. Robert knew that for the first time in his life he was staring into the face of extreme poverty. He could see that simply keeping warm would be a major accomplishment in winter. He thought of his own comfortable surroundings and almost felt fortunate. A slight twinge of conscience pricked at him, but he quickly shoved it aside.

Then his attention turned to Willa, still flustered and remiss to interrupt his inspection. He carefully observed her shapely body accentuated by the cheap clothes she was wearing. Instantly, he turned and peered toward the curtained door. "Is the baby in here?"

"Uh, yes she is," Willa said and headed for the kitchen. She drew back the curtains and escorted the doctor into her tiny kitchen. A two-burner oil stove with a portable tin oven sat in one corner beside four whitewashed orange crates stacked and nailed together, serving as cabinets. A wooden table, with two crude benches tucked underneath, ruled the middle of the uneven floor. The table covering and the curtains on the tiny window facing the river were both marked by meticulously embroidered borders. Even to Robert, it was apparent that great effort was put forth to make this hovel into a home. Robert's eyes finally came to rest on a second, somewhat larger bed nestled against the inner wall where Aster lay napping.

Willa had not spoken a word since he had entered the kitchen. She watched him intently with the same wild, sensual cat-like awareness he had seen in his office.

"May I?" He said, pointing to the bed.

"Of course," she murmured.

Robert took the stethoscope from his medical bag. Intently, he listened to Aster's breathing.

Without looking up, he announced, "There's been a new outbreak of influenza in the county. I was concerned for Aster, although she seems to be doing just fine." He replaced the stethoscope into his bag and faced her. "How does Friday sound to you?"

"Friday?" She faltered.

"As a work day. I prefer Fridays," he continued, "but if that's not satisfactory, another day will do fine. That is, if you're interested," he said casually. "There's a possibility that we might make this a permanent arrangement." Hope leaped into her eyes as he suspected it would.

Without thinking, Willa seized his hand. "Oh yes," she breathed. "Thank you, thank you so much!" She was suddenly aware of how warm and solid his hand felt within hers. Instantly, she dropped it. In spite of the chill in the room, she began to feel a warm glow.

Robert sensed he had tarried long enough. He picked up the medical bag and walked out of the kitchen and to the front door. Before opening it, he turned to face her. "While I'm down here, do you know of anyone needing my services?"

"Merna Higgers and most of her children are sick," Willa responded.

Long after Robert had disappeared through the door, Willa simply stared at it. An involuntary shiver ran through her. "The devil has just walked over my grave," she said out of habit, then went back about the business of trying to keep warm.

Old Bean slithered from underneath the house. He crouched on his haunches and growled as Robert approached Little Son Higgers' shack. Keeping one eye on the dog, Robert knocked on the door.

Bean growled again, this time baring his teeth.

Little Son opened the door with one hand. In his other hand he held a bottle of Nash's Chill Tonic.

"Little Son?" Robert asked.

The hellhound's growl grew louder.

"Ya'nt," Little Son said. He stepped outside and closed the door. "Old Bean here is a coon dog," he said, nodding in Bean's direction. "He'll hunt with might neer anyone, but he don't seem to like you none."

"At the moment, the feeling is mutual," Robert replied bluntly. "I was just over checking on the Sinclair baby. Mrs. Sinclair told me you have sickness in your family. Since flu's spreading across Dunklin County, I felt I should check on your family while I'm here."

Little Son hesitated for a few seconds. A child's cough rattled from inside the house. Little Son stared back at the closed door. Robert could tell from the expression on his face that he was concerned about his family. Still, Little Son hesitated, staring at the Nash's Chill Tonic he held in his hand. The two drops of turpentine and sugar he'd been giving the little ones simply hadn't stopped their coughing. For the last hour he'd been studyin' on givin'em a dose of Castor Oil. No sir, he just couldn't bring himself to turn the doctor away. "I reckon we could use yore help," he said, throwing open the door to the foul smelling shack.

After Robert had finished with the children, Little Son asked, "How about some ree-freshments? I got a pot of fresh coffee and you never can tell, I just might find a little something to go in it." Little Son waved Robert to a bench under the kitchen table. A giant cooking stove sat against the outer wall, with the stovepipe poking out a broken window. Set off to one side was an iron skillet with cold gravy caked down its side. An extra long beat-up table, still strewn with the remains of the morning meal, dominated the room. Crude shelves, serving various purposes, lined the walls. The rest of the room was littered with beds containing sick children.

While the chubby little man went about the business of getting two cups and pouring the coffee, Robert carefully observed his surroundings. If the twins were making illegal whiskey in their home as he had heard, he couldn't see any signs of it. From the smell, however, he could tell there was a crock of something fermenting in the corner.

Little Son pulled out one of the benches. "Make yore self ta home, Doc." He waddled across the kitchen. When he returned, he had a fruit jar in his hand. "The sump'n extry I mentioned." He winked at Robert and whispered in a conspiring manner, "I gotta little special brew jest finishin' up over in the corner. I plan to see that you git some soon as she's ready." He proceeded to lace Robert's coffee and then his own with a goodly amount from the jar. "Cain't sample her too soon or hit'll give you the trots."

"What is it?" Robert ventured to ask.

"Homemade brew."

"Really," Robert said as if astonished by the subject.

"You never heard of homemade brew, Doc?"

Robert shook his head.

"Why you can jest about make homemade brew out'a anything. You take a little sugar and some malt. Add a big old Irish tater if you want a bigger kick. Put it all in a crock of water. Add some yeast and wait until she starts to bubble. That's when you sweet'n' her agin. That's all there is to it."

Robert forced down the cup of coffee and walked to the door to leave. He hesitated for a second and then asked, "What about that dog?"

"Awe, there ain't no need to worry none about old Bean," Little Son said, giving the dog a dismissive wave. "All you gotta do is look him in the eye and tell'em 'Go to hell, Bean,' and he will."

Chapter 13
In Good Faith

"Where in the hell do you think you're goin'?" John growled, not that he really gave a damn about what Willa did. As usual, he felt like shit and wanted to take his nastiness out on someone.

Willa ignored him for several moments. Well, I guess he has to know sooner or later, she thought. She placed her coat and hat on the foot of the bed and turned to face him. "I have a job, J-O-B. Since you are not familiar with the idea, I'll try to explain it to you. A job means that you agree to do something for someone in exchange for money. This is called work, W-O-R-K." She paused. "Tell me John, have you ever done a lick of work in your entire life?"

"Work!" John grunted. "Who in the hell'd hire you? You don't know nothing about doin' a damn thing 'cept diddlin'. Come to think of it, you ain't no good at that!"

Willa listened to his malicious words without the slightest show of emotion. She calmly put on her coat and hat. In this situation, the urge to brag was stronger than her feeling of indifference.

"Not that it is any of your business," she stated, "but I will be working for the new doctor."

John laughed and slapped the table. "That fancy pants? Me and Rabbit, we seen 'em the day he come into town. Hell! He ain't no doctor. Doctors get their hands dirty. He looks more like a damn matinee idol. I bet he thinks he is one, too."

Willa shrugged her shoulders and smiled. "You should know," she said sarcastically.

"Go to hell," he said.

Willa put on her coat and hat, covered Aster with a blanket, placed her on her hip and headed for the door. "Oh, I don't have to leave home to do that, John. We live in hell. You just don't have sense enough to know it." With a sense of satisfaction that she had not felt in a long time, Willa walked out of the back door of the shack. After dropping the baby off at her parent's house, she took a deep breath and steeled herself against the long, cold walk to town.

Having failed to get in the last word, a spasm of irritation crossed John's face, only to be replaced by a look of gleeful anticipation. If she really had a job, money would be coming into the house. Without a doubt, he would manage to get part of it.

Willa straightened her hat, pulled a handkerchief from her purse, and blew her cold red nose. Nervously she slipped onto the back porch of Robert's house. Several seconds passed before she got up enough nerve to knock.

Robert, wearing a pair of cashmere herringbone weave trousers and a white linen shirt, opened the kitchen door. A handmade silk tie showed from underneath a double-breasted vest of contrasting flannel.

Although Willa had worn her best, she knew that next to him she must appear dowdy in her brown tweed coat and wine-colored mushroom hat. For a second, she wished the floor would open and swallow her up. You Ninny, she scolded, what difference does it make to him how you dressed? Taking a deep breath and crossing the threshold, Willa Sinclair changed her life forever.

. Showing her the utility closet, Robert said. "You may place your belongings in here."

Self-consciously, Willa did as he said, revealing to him in all his elegance, a green wool sweater that, despite its condition, accented her hazel eyes and wind blown chestnut-colored hair. A black rayon pleated skirt, slick from too many pressings, plus a pair of well-worn black oxfords and mended hose completed her attire.

While Willa hung her coat, Robert surveyed every inch of her body and congratulated himself on finding such a natural beauty; one that even pathetic clothing could not hide. Guilt surfaced due to the trap he was baiting for her. As quickly as it came, he abandoned it. What the hell did he care? She couldn't possibly be any worse off. If anything, his attention would be a blessing. He intended to pay her well for her services, didn't he?

By the time he had given her a few menial instructions, his blue eyes had turned as cold as steel.

Moments later, he settled into his car. Before he started the engine, he studied the entrance to the house. "She is exactly what the doctor ordered," he said in a whisper. "But I must have some patience." Realizing that patience was not one of his virtues; he gave a long sigh. "Assuming," he said with a sneer, "that I have any virtues at all." Cranking the engine, he put the Packard in gear and backed out of the driveway.

Robert would have liked to stay longer with Willa, but he was on his way to the Holler. This time he was going by invitation.

Little Son got down on his knees, and slowly handed the fruit jars full of whiskey through the hole in the kitchen floor to Big Boy. When they had finished, Little Son extended his hand to pull Big Boy out of the hole.

"You know the doc is up to sump'em, don't che? Why else would he want to talk to us?" Big Boy asked, once he was out of the hole. "You don't reckon he's got anything to do with them revenuers, do ye?"

Little Son scoffed. "Hell, we ain't worth them goin' to that much trouble. If we wuz gettin' rich down here, they might come after us. A feller can't get rich bootleggin' anymore." He pulled his hat off and used it to knock the dust from his overalls.

"That's what you told'em, so why would he insist on talkin' about it?" Big Boy asked.

"Yore guess is as good as mine." Little Son made a clicking sound with his tongue. "I don't think he cares about makin' money. Maybe it's the excitement he's after. He ain't been here but a few months, and Jay Sky says he's already bored, and for some reason, he cain't leave. I'm about to think that myself. In any case we'll know soon enough. What'che say we give him a little test?" he added, giving Little Son a sly wink.

Bean saw Robert coming. He hunkered down under the edge of the front porch and growled.

Robert, leery of the dog despite what Little Son had told him, somehow managed to muster up enough courage to stare the dog down. "Go to hell, Bean," he said in a stern voice. Bean whimpered, tucked his tail, and crawled under the house. Robert mounted the rickety steps and knocked.

"Howdy, Doc," Big Boy said. "You jest in time fer some breakfast. Come on in," he announced, making several beckoning gestures with his chubby arm.

Robert entered the kitchen to see that the extra long table that dominated the room, with its soiled oilcloth, was laden with an odd assortment of dishes, in the middle of which sat a huge bowl of gravy. Beside the gravy was a platter of fried fatback floating in grease.

Verna Higgers waddled across the floor carrying a giant pan of biscuits. She placed the biscuits on the table, then using the back of her hand she swiped at the snuff running down her chin. Rubbing it off on her hip, she gave a jolly laugh that caused her belly to shake. "You gonna be jest like old Doc Wilson, I can see that. He always liked my cookin'. I use ta feed him a lot." She shooed the children over on one of the long benches, and somehow managed to squeeze Robert in beside Pebo.

Pebo grinned affably. "How's yore mama doin'?" he whispered.

Verna hurried across the kitchen as fast as her short legs and plump body would allow and poured him a tin cup of coffee. Two of the younger boys got into a scuffle on the other side of the table. Big Boy raised himself and offered to backhand both of them if they didn't shut up.

"Them two is always causin' devilment," Verna offered. She took it upon herself to fill Robert's plate. When she finished, she gave the nod. The boys grabbed at the food with both hands. When they finished, they wiped their mouths on the back of their hands and then rubbed their hands on the side of their pants. They took turns at the water bucket to wash down the greasy breakfast.

"Mind you don't spill it on the floor," Verna cautioned.

Passing the dipper from one to another, they carefully leaned forward, making certain that any spills or dribbles fell back into the water bucket.

"Com'on Doc, eat up," Big Boy encouraged. He gave several jabs of his fork, pointing to the over-flowing plate in front of Robert.

Robert's eyes zeroed in on the piece of flypaper hanging from the ceiling. Directly under the flypaper sat the bowl that had been, up to a few moments ago, brimming with gravy. Robert swallowed. His eyes moved back and forth from the flies to the bowl.

Big Boy stopped eating and watched in silence.

It suddenly occurred to Robert that he was being tested. He looked at the plate before him and thought of the consequences that should he alienate the Higgers. What the hell, he thought, as he picked up his fork and dug in.

Shortly after breakfast, Little Son joined them, and Robert laid out his plans.

"We'll think on it and let you know," the twins said.

Robert raised his tall, lean body from the uncomfortable bench and made his good-byes. From the look on the twin's face, he felt he had made a good impression.

Big Boy and Verna Higgers watched Robert go. Big Boy nodded his head and hugged his square little wife. "He's comin' along good, Vernie, don't ye think? If we work on him, he might make us a pertly good doc yet." Big Boy turned back to the table, picked up the empty gravy bowl, and placed it on the floor in front of Bean. "Ain't that right, Bean?"

The children stopped what they were doing and all eyes turned to Bean.

Big Boy leaned down and gave the dog a somber look. "Ya'nt, ya'nt, Bean," he said. "I'll tell'em word fer word, you can count on it."

"Whut did he say?" they all sang out.

Big Boy sighed. "Bean ain't much of a believer. He's a true Mizzoury-ite if I ever seed one. Ye jest gotta show'em first." He shook his head as if disgusted by what the dog had to say. "Old Bean said he reckoned we was going to do what we wanted to but the best ad-vice he could give us about the new doctor is not to go countin' our chickens 'fore they hatch."

Verna turned to her husband with a censorious look on her face.

"I know, Vernie, that ain't really whut Bean said," Big Boy whispered with wide-eyed innocence. "I think it's time you had a talk with that dog about the language he's been usin' lately."

Willa drifted through her strange New World as lost as Alice in Wonderland. Moving carefully through the dining room, she cautiously eyed the exquisite Tiffany china. Entering the bedroom, she finally got up enough nerve to finger a deluxe vanity set, consisting of an atomizer, a powder box of orchid enamel with a gold luster design, all resting on a matching tray. It was definitely a feminine article. With a twinge of envy, she wondered about the owner.

Above all else, the bathroom fascinated the poverty-stricken young woman, who in her entire life had never had the luxury of languishing in a full bath. For a few seconds, she tantalized herself with the thought of running the big tub full of hot water and climbing into it. Of course, she would never take such a liberty. She lifted a bottle of Halo shampoo from the edge of the tub, smelled it, and quickly replaced the cap as a sense of guilt overwhelmed her. After setting it in its proper place, she placed her finger on her chin. There was one more thing that spiked her curiosity. She simply must see how store-bought soap smelled. She lifted the bar of Ivory bath soap lying in the soap dish and breathed deeply of its bouquet. "Well," she stated in satisfaction, "it don't smell any better than Mama's."

Back in the kitchen, she dragged the contraption that he had called a vacuum cleaner out of the closet. "Now," she stated, "if I can just figger out how to make this thing work, I'll clean up this place."

When all her chores were complete, Willa finally looked in the cookie jar where he had said he left her money. She gasped. He had left her five dollars for just a few hours! Why that was double the money that she could earn all day picking cotton.

On her way home, she contemplated her dilemma. Should she spend any of the money before she paid her doctor bill? Temptation got the better of her. It had been such a long time since she and Aster had had a treat. She stopped at Mays' Grocery and bought a pound of bologna, a loaf of light bread, a Pepsi-Cola for herself, a pound of coffee for Ben and Effie, and a quart of sweet milk for Aster. Then she bought something special for them all, a Hostess Twinkie. Despite John, life was as close to wonderful as it had ever been for Willa Sinclair.

Chapter 14
In Broad Daylight

A few weeks later Willa entered Robert's house with the confidence built through his trust and her ability to earn her own living. She strolled across the kitchen floor. In the hall, she leaned into the mirror to study her reflection. The colors in her new dress, with its peasant border print, made her hazel eyes appear green. She had the kind of eyes that men liked, or so her friend Ruby had told her. But would someone as sophisticated and worldly as Robert Vaughn notice? The part of her that made sense when she listened warned her against this kind of thinking. No sooner did the admonition enter her head than she discarded it. What did it really matter? She was living her ultimate fantasy. Here she was the beautiful Cinderella and he a Prince Charming.

Willa ran her fingers through her hair. She was thinking of having it bobbed. Papa said no. A woman's hair is her crowning glory. But Papa's just old- fashioned, she told herself as she gathered her long tresses into a bun. She wondered what Robert's thoughts were about a woman's hair. Did he prefer long hair or short hair? She let her hands travel over her body. Cupping a breast in each hand, she preened first this way and then that as she admired the way her bosom occupied the front of the dress. "Shame on you, Willa. Those were silly thoughts, and you know very well what Mama would say if she knew you were having them."

After selecting an assortment of cleaning supplies, Willa carried them to the sink to fill the bucket with water. She was about to add the cleaner when the hairs on the back of her neck stirred. She whirled to find Robert standing in the doorway. Having been scared out of her wits, she suddenly felt faint and, without realizing it, reeled to one side.

Robert was across the room in a flash, supporting her.

Dreaming was one thing in which Willa would freely admit she overindulged. Deep down inside of her, the actuality of having her dreams come true had never crossed her mind. A dozen thoughts raced through her head, none made any sense until a sobering thought told her that he was still home merely because he had overslept. And, of course, the only explanation for him holding her was because she had almost fallen.

"I'm sorry," she whispered, in a strangled voice. After making an attempt to clear her throat, she went on, "you startled me."

"There's no reason to be sorry," he said.

Willa was suddenly aware of how close they were and just how his body was touching hers. She took a deep breath and waited for him to release her. When he didn't, she tried to move away, or did she? She opened her mouth to speak.

"Don't talk," he whispered. "Just let me make love to you."

Never taking his eyes off hers, he cradled the back of her head in his hands and slowly lowered his mouth. Her scent enveloped him, captivating him. He'd known women, but none of them had smelled like this one. "Sweet," he murmured, "so sweet."

His mouth came down on hers, fierce, hot and demanding. As his kiss shot through her senses, Willa couldn't help but wrap her arms around his neck as she sank deeper and deeper into the swirl of sensual delight. Eagerly, his kisses, along with his hands, moved over her body until her clothing slithered its way down her torso like a snake shedding its skin. This should not be happening, she thought. He took the nipples of her breast, first one and then the other into his mouth. Her eyes gleamed with astonished wonder, as the desire for him enhanced and spread like warm honey throughout her body. Instinctively, Willa arched her back and thrust herself forward. The action was instantly followed by shame, so much so that she wanted to die.

Over and over his viperous tongue flicked from one point to the other until she was ready to relinquish herself completely. He beckoned her to the bedroom. Like a starving kitten after a bowl of warm milk, she followed.

There, he found the contours of her body eminently satisfying. *As though she were made for me…*Something akin to a severe pain ripped though his body. Stiffening, he reeled to a stop, rolled to the far side of the bed and broke into a cold sweat. Cursing severely, he rolled once more, this time in Willa's direction and straddled her. In one quick motion, he grasped the hair on both sides of her head and held her firmly against the bed…

Robert lay on his stomach for several long seconds with his face pressed into the pillow, groaning as if he were in pain. Without a word of explanation, he sprang to his feet, entered the bathroom, and slammed the door.

No matter how many times Willa commanded her body to move it simply refused to obey her. The sound of the outer door opening and Robert leaving the house gave her the strength she needed to drag herself to her feet and then into the bathroom. Gripping the sides of the porcelain sink for support, she stared at the giant tub. A bizarre thought crossed her mind that maybe she could scrub all that had happened away. Filling the tub, and without fascination, Willa lowered her body into the steaming water. Rocking back and forth, she cursed first Robert and then herself. "Damn you, Willa!" Burying her face in her hands, she sobbed. "What will I do now?" The money had been so good, and she so desperately needed the job.

Willa's head came up with a jerk. "Money!" she repeated. "He thinks he's paying for my services. How dumb can I be?" Bolting upright in the tub, she screamed, "There ain't no way in hell that I'm going to tuck my tail and run away." *Willa girl,* she could just hear Ruby Wilkerson say. *Being from the Holler comes with a money back guarantee that states life is sure as hell gonna shit on you one way or another. You can't stop it from happening, but you damn sure don't have to let it be rubbed in. There's a trick to it my friend, when are you gonna wise up?*

"Good Heavens!" she declared, suddenly realizing Ruby's meaning. "And what am I doing? I'm sitting here, the blue hen's chicken, with my tail feathers wet and drooping to my knees." At that point her eyes rested on the bottle of Halo shampoo.

"Why not?"

After helping herself to everything she could find, including administering a dab of manly cologne behind each ear, she stared at the reflection of herself in the mirror over the basin. Leaning toward her image, she said, "We've learned a lot since the last time we had a talk, haven't we?" Walking into the bedroom, she stared at the tumbled-up bed. There must be a way to get even with him. Throwing the hairbrush against the wall, she said, "Yes, oh yes," with more determination than she had ever felt in her young life, she declared. "I can find a way."

Chapter 15
In Close Proximity

For over two hours, District Attorney James Horner Shaw had diligently applied himself to a murder case. Some idiot living in the backwoods had taken a stick of stove wood and battered in the head of his father-in-law while the old man slept in his bed. A good old man, James thought. He had known him all of his life, and he intended to see that the imbecile paid for his crime.

Shaw rubbed his aching neck, then nestled his head into the back of the well-defined indent that years of prior use had made into the soft leather of the swivel-backed chair. Shaw pushed himself away from the massive mahogany desk and gazed around the familiar office. It had been his father's law office and his grandfather's before him, a solid, warm, and friendly place. Some folks might describe it as a bit old fashioned. Shaw preferred to think of it as having mellowed to the years with age. To tell the truth, he liked it that way. After the last election when he'd become the district attorney for Dunklin County, the thought had crossed his mind that he could save time by packing up and moving to Kennett, Missouri, the county seat. Deep down though, Shaw knew that he could never bring himself to move, any more than he could bring himself to redecorate. After all, it was his great-grandfather, in 1840, who hacked his way through the wilderness from Tennessee to establish Horner's Landing, as it was called back then.

Shaw sighed and looked at his watch, then did what he always did after noting the time of the day—he swiveled around to check on the noonday traffic. Traffic was at a minimum, due to the weather, he supposed. James tapped his fingers on the desktop and reckoned to himself that he was about as habitual as a man could get.

He donned his coat and hat. Glancing at his reflection in the long mirror beside the front door, he realized he was still a rather young man. Never had he been what one would call handsome, but when he was interested, he had attracted his faire share of the opposite sex. In his youth he had been told the gals went for his head of thick auburn hair and soft amber eyes, not to mention a smile that his mother always said could melt ice. Some said he needed to get himself a life outside of the law, find a good woman, and marry. But he reckoned he didn't want to anymore. Jurisprudence had taken center stage in his life.

Shaw left his office and hunched his shoulders against the weather. Opening the door to the City Café, he was greeted by the familiar aroma of country cooking. There was a faint hum of talk and laughter coming from a group seated just inside the left-hand corner where four of the patrons were engrossed in a game of dominoes.

Out of habit, James inquired. "Who's winning?"

"Frances," the male voices answered in unison.

Shaw nodded. He didn't know why he bothered to ask, because Frances was always beating the hell out of these guys. He exchanged howdy's with several other patrons before seating himself in his favorite spot.

"The usual, Mr. Shaw?" Sherry Thomas, the owner's redheaded daughter inquired.

"Why not?" James replied.

"No reason," she said. Placing a glass of iced tea in front of him, she gave him a sly smile, then bent down and whispered in his ear.

"Daddy said it would probably bust your gut if you were to eat anything different."

Shaw laughed. "Smart man, your daddy. You tell him I said if he keeps on he'll soon be as smart as your mama."

Sherry rolled her eyes. "Now that is a facetious statement if I ever heard one. You know there ain't nobody as smart as my mama." She patted James's shoulder, "Hot roast beef, creamed potatoes, and black-eyed peas, coming up."

I like that girl, James thought. She makes an admirable opponent.

Sherry brought James's lunch, which he ate without pause in silence. When he finally glanced up, he saw Robert Vaughn enter the café. James' eyes, darting around the room, picked up no empty tables. Having just recently heard how the doctor made several charity calls on the needy of the Holler, he felt guilty for having prejudged the man and not having made his acquaintance. He felt obliged to do something he normally didn't do—share his table. He sighed, pushed back his chair, stood up, and approached Robert.

"My name is James Shaw. You're welcome to join me if you like," he said as he extended his hand.

A look of surprise crossed Robert's face. He shook Shaw's hand. "Thank you," he said.

The two men walked to the table. Robert slid into the chair opposite James.

Trying to open a line of communication, James groped around for a subject.

"Damn cold out today," he stated after an awkward silence.

Robert nodded his head in agreement, but didn't comment.

He's not going to make this easy, James thought.

Sherry replenished James's tea, then concentrated on Robert. "What will you have today, Doctor?"

Robert studied the menu. "Well, young lady, I believe I'll try the beef stew."

"Thank you," Sherry replied, and briskly walked away.

"I owe you an apology, sir," James said straight out. "I should have made your acquaintance before now."

"I'm sure you've been busy," Robert offered half heartily. "I've been following the murder case."

"I've been busy alright," he said, "but that's no excuse for ill manners."

During a very slowly eaten lunch, the two men had a lengthy discussion about their respective professions. Shaw realized that under the cocky manner, Robert Vaughn was quite an interesting man, and that he enjoyed his company. Before leaving the café that day, the two men agreed to have lunch together as often as possible.

Chapter 16
With Intent

Vengeance is mine, sayeth the Lord. For as long as she could remember, Willa had known the quote from the Bible. The hell-fire and damnation preached in the Holler had served warning that, should she go against God's teachings, he could, anytime he pleased, reach down from the heavens and smite her.

Despite her fears, Willa left the Holler at sunup. At Robert Vaughn's backdoor, she bowed her head one last time. "I know what I'm about to do ain't right, Lord, so I'm asking you, right here and now for one last time to forgive me. Please, Lord," she pleaded, "try to understand." She took a deep breath, squared her shoulders, and cautiously opened the door. Placing her belongings in the closet, she glanced around the kitchen and decided the best way to avoid suspicion was to go about her normal routine.

After several moments of tidying up, she grabbed the bundle of clean shirts that had arrived from the cleaners and made her way down the hall toward the bedroom. Pausing, she gave herself another piece of advice, act the nitwit that he thinks you are. Opening the bedroom door, she crossed the room to the armoire. No sooner had she placed the shirts inside, than she heard the bathroom door open. The wispy sounds of his bare feet scraping the carpet reached her ears. Cold chills ran up her spine. Resisting the impulse to shiver, Willa steeled herself to remain perfectly still. Every nerve in her body was strained to the point of exploding. The wispy sounds grew louder until she felt his hand on her shoulder.

Willa Sinclair took a deep breath, placed her left hand in the palm of her right, and with all the strength she possessed, used her right elbow to give him a reverberating whack in his ribs.

Robert gasped with pain, clutched his side, and stumbled backward. Collapsing onto the bed, he rolled from side to side before curling himself into a ball. It was several long seconds before he could speak.

"What in the hell do you think you're doing?" he managed to groan.

"I just punched you, and I'll do it again if you get off of that bed," Willa declared, hopefully, she was sounding braver than she felt. Taking a deep breath, she searched the room with her eyes for added protection.

Robert, speechless for the moment, could only stare at the young woman to whom he had vowed to be passive.

"We need to get something straight," she added. Grabbing up one of his well-polished shoes, she wagged it in his direction. "You seem to have gotten the impression somewhere along the line that you've bought and paid for me. But that's not the case. I only agreed to be your housekeeper, nothing more." Without giving Robert time to answer, she continued. "So we need to understand something right here and now, Mr. High and Mighty. Regardless of the differences in our circumstances, I cannot be bought. I don't care how much money you dangle in front of me. Do you understand me? I *ain't*, and never will be, yours or anyone's whore!"

Robert sneered, despite the pain in his side. He did the best he could to produce a nasty-sounding laugh. "You mean to tell me you never had a clue? You may be dumb, but I hardly think that even you are that dumb." His remark hurt. He could see it in her eyes.

Willa slung the shoe at his head. "Then you're not all that bright yourself, Buster," she spewed out, and headed for the kitchen.

Having fended off the shoe with his forearm, Robert groaned and rolled to his feet to follow her. "You appeared willing enough," he scoffed.

From down the hall came the response, "Willing to be…to be at your service? To be used depending on whatever kind of mood that you happen to be in? Not on your life, buddy! You ain't got that kind'a money, nor has anyone else for that matter." Flinging open the closet door, she jerked so hard on her coat that it sent the hanger hurling across the room. Blinded by rage, she marched across the kitchen toward the back door, fumbling to insert her arm into the coat sleeve as she went.

Robert, for reasons he did not understand, found it virtually impossible to let her walk out of his life. Limping after her, he jerked the coat from her hands, returned it to the closet, and slammed the door with the same intensity in which Willa had opened it. Groaning from the effort, he grasped his bruise, gave her one last glare, and stomped down the hall to the bedroom.

Stunned at his actions, Willa found herself momentarily confused. Placing her hands on her hips, she paced the room, wondering if she should *git* while the *git'n*'s good, as her mama would say. No, she was still mad, damn mad. She'd never felt such exhilaration, and she damn well intended to see this through.

Several moments passed before Robert stalked back into the kitchen, this time fully dressed, although not quite up to his usual impeccable standards. With one arm wrapped securely around his rib cage, he threw Willa a scorching look before hurling himself out the back door.

"Well? Well!" she stated. Throwing up her hands in amazement, she dropped into a nearby chair and stared at the back door. For the first time, she realized the possible consequences of her actions. "Well, it didn't happen," she stated flatly, "and thank you, Lord, for that." But she wondered why he didn't fire her. She fully expected him to. "Too late to start worrying about that now," she said. With a critical eye, she surveyed the kitchen.

"I love this room," she stated. With pleasure she recalled how she had worked to give it a used look despite the fact that there was very little, if any, cooking going on there.

"I reckon, since he didn't fire me," she told the tiny plant in the window, "I'll just do my work, collect my money, and then be on my way."

For the next hour, Willa went about doing what little needed to be done. When she finished, she walked from room to room, committing the sights to memory. She hated the thought of returning to the days of not having a dime to her name. Most of all, she hated not being able to provide for Aster.

Before preparing to leave, she opened the cookie jar where Robert regularly left her wages. Instead of the usual five-dollar bill, she found a wad of bills amounting to twenty-five dollars. She scoffed at the additional money, took only the five dollars which she had earned. Giving the thirsty houseplant a drink of water, she stroked the tender new leaves. "Good-bye little plant," she said softly. Putting on her coat and hat, she reached for the door handle but paused and pivoted on her heels. She walked back to face the plant and declared with determination, "That was in case he fires me. If he doesn't, I'll see you next Friday."

That evening when John made an appearance at the shack, he found himself removed, lock, stock, and barrel, from the house to the chicken coop in the backyard. In John's case, the possessions thrown from the house amounted to a paper bag and a cardboard box of old clothes and junk.

"What am I going to do?" He whined.

Willa's upper lip curled in contempt. "You can pick shit with the chickens for all I care."

The week passed without Willa hearing a word from Robert. On Friday, she returned to work as though nothing had happened and found that he was nowhere in sight.

Winter passed into spring and then summer without incident, but the silent conflict that raged between Willa Sinclair and Robert Vaughn continued.

Robert stood at the edge of the Holler and once again asked himself the same question he had asked over and over since the day of the fiasco with Willa. Why had he ruined it? His eyes automatically scanned the tiny shack where Willa lived. Noting the light in the kitchen, he slowly made his way across the Holler.

Well before dawn, Willa Sinclair found herself, yet again, pacing the water-warped floor of the tiny kitchen. Despite her best effort to be as quiet as possible, the boards creaked. Aster stirred. Pausing, she held her breath until the baby settled down. Creeping to the window, she placed her forehead against the cool pane and closed her eyes. "Foolish, foolish girl," she chided bitterly. "I've gotten my hind-end kicked good and proper and yet I can't stop thinking about him."

Willa opened the window. Leaning on her elbows, she took a deep breath of the cool fall air. It was several seconds before she saw Robert through the mist. She closed the window as quickly as she had opened it and stepped back into the shadows.

Justin Rider saw it all. "Why don't you leave her alone?" he demanded.

Rider's sudden appearance gave Robert a start. He quickly composed himself, turned, and feigned surprise. "What makes you think there is any need for me to, as you put it, to leave Mrs. Sinclair alone?"

Justin snorted. "I don't believe it's the bootlegging or the scenery that keeps you coming down here so often. That is unless, of course, you consider Willa Sinclair part of the scenery."

"I don't consider Mrs. Sinclair anything," Robert snapped. "Nor do I consider my relationship with her, or anyone else down here for that matter, any of your concern."

"As far as the twins go, you're right, it isn't any of my business." Justin conceded. "But Willa is family; that makes her my concern." Then he added, "Life has already dealt her more than her share of pain. Find what you and I both know you are after someplace other than the Holler."

Robert made a vague sound of annoyance. "How could you possibly know what I want?" After a pause in which he tried to find a phrase to defend himself, he added, "Money doesn't buy everything a man needs or seeks." The words were no sooner out his mouth than he asked himself, what was that supposed to mean?

"Down here money is everything. Life or death can literally depend on a lot less than what you pay to have your shirt laundered. Why are you in Hornersville in the first place?" Justin demanded.

Robert grunted. "You mean you haven't heard? I'm the town physician," he said with as much sarcasm as he could muster.

"So you are," Justin said. "Remember one thing, physician, when you're in the Holler, you're in my territory, and I'll be watching you."

Robert's lips curled. "Watch all you want, Rider. I don't have anything to hide." Robert walked away, leaving Justin to stare after him. On the way to the car, he admonished himself for visiting the Holler far too often.

Willa had asked herself the same question that Robert asked of himself—why? Why had he offered her so much, then in the same breath, snatched it away? What troubled her even more was that despite everything, she still dreamed about how it might have been. Her only solace in the early morning hours was that if at sometime in the near future she made the decision to pursue the promise, somehow she would have to make him suffer in the process. What she needed was a plan of action. "Yes," she stated, "a plan of action...I must think of one."

Justin Rider had promised the day to Pebo. But despite his best efforts to enjoy their little fishing expedition, he couldn't keep from thinking about Ruby and the promise he had seen in her eyes earlier that morning when she ran her finger down his cheek.

How about spending this afternoon with me? Ruby had said, licking her full red lips. *We could take a little boat ride if you'd like.*

Would he like? Justin drooled just thinking about it. But having promised Pebo, he had reluctantly declined her offer. When he couldn't stand it any longer, he clapped Pebo on the back. "Pebo buddy," he said, "I just remembered that I have something very important that I need to do today."

Pebo blinked in surprise. "Huh, okay, okay," he said as he gathered up his fishing gear.

Fearing that Pebo would assuredly want to tag along, Justin added, "Why don't you stay here? If you'll catch some fish, I'll fry them for supper. "

Pebo shook his head no. He loved fishing, and he loved eating fish, but he loved spending time with Jay Sky even more.

Justin had to think fast. "Do you remember the last lesson we had about thinking for yourself?"

Pebo didn't really remember, but he said he did.

"If I said to you, Pebo, go jump in the river, what would you do?"

Pebo glanced around. He didn't know why Jay Sky wanted him to jump in the river. He had already done it that morning, and he didn't think he smelled bad yet. He shrugged his shoulders and bent forward to untie his shoelaces.

"Hold on," Justin laughed, "*don't* do that. Listen to me. You took a bath this morning, didn't you?"

Pebo nodded.

"So why do it again so soon?"

Pebo looked bewildered. He didn't understand why Jay Sky would tell him to do something, then in the same breath tell him not to do it.

Was Jay Sky trying to make him mad? Pebo's face took on the obstinate look of a child. "Cause *you* said."

"What if someone other than me told you to do it, would you?"

"Noo-pe."

"Good," Justin said, "Why wouldn't you do it?"

"Cause I already done it."

"Exactly!" Justin exclaimed. "That's all I want you to do, buddy, is to think for yourself. So think now...remember, you *don't* have to stop fishing...if you *don't* want to."

Pebo's brow wrinkled in concentration. Don't, don't. Jay Sky was always tellin' him "don't". He didn't want to disappoint his best friend in all the world. So what was he gonna do?

Justin patiently watched as the expression on Pebo's face suddenly changed to one of enlightenment.

Pebo straightened himself up and with a grin that reached from ear to ear, he announced, "Cause I don't want to."

For a second Justin looked as stunned as Pebo looked happy. Then he burst into laughter and laughed until Pebo joined in, relieved that he had somehow pleased Jay Sky. At last, Justin got a hold of his emotions and wiped his eyes. Unknowingly, simple Pebo had just outsmarted him.

"Good boy," he managed to say. Then together...they headed for home.

"Morning, John," Justin said dryly.

John Sinclair hid his bottle, pulled himself to his feet, and staggered out of the thicket.

The shine-still was in operation, and John was on surveillance. As far as John was concerned, it was a job made for him. All that was required was to move up and down the river for about a mile. Mostly he sat and drank and did very little surveillance. The twins had warned him several times about drinking "on the job." John Sinclair knew he had an easy job, and he knew why he had it.

"Damn-sons-a-bitches!" he told his friend Rabbit that morning. "They ain't about to fire me. I know too much. They ain't foolin' old John. They hired me for no other reason than to keep my mouth shut. Then they put me away off down here and tell me to watch. Like I don't know that there ain't no way in hell that any feller could get past the first three men."

He waited until Justin and Pebo were out of sight. Throwing a few choice words in their direction, John slipped back into the thicket, found his bottle, and sat back against a tree. He had another swallow for good measure.

"Yep, old John ain't the fool they think he is. John knows a lot of things they think he don't know, a lot of things," he repeated, laid his head back and began to snore.

Chapter 17
Motive for an Act

Just about the only month that anything new happened around Hornersville was in September. One by one the carnival trucks rolled across the railroad tracks and maneuvered their way down Main Street, ending their trek in the vacant lot between the doctor's office and city hall.

As always, the annual event created an excitement that was contagious. As Justin Rider strolled down the street, everyone he met had a comment to make about the festivities. He stopped in front of the post office long enough to observe several old men sitting on the benches. They called out from time to time bits of advice to the roustabouts on how to best assemble the rides. When the carnies didn't listen, they declared that like all young'uns of today, they didn't know and wouldn't listen to a damn thing.

As Justin watched, his thoughts turned to Willa, who had been down in the dumps for several weeks. He saw the carnival as a good opportunity to pull her out of it.

"Let's take in the carnival tonight, Willa," he said eagerly.

"I don't know," she said.

"Come on now," Justin admonished. "You know we always take the kids. How can you disappoint them?"

"Wee—ll, okay," Willa answered as listlessly as possible. Then she perked up a little. She still hadn't worn the new dress from Sears and Roebuck that she had been saving for a special occasion.

Willa placed the flat iron on the stove to heat. Spitting on her finger, she quickly touched the bottom of the iron. The sizzling sound assured her the iron was hot and ready for use. Placing a quilt on top of the table, she began to press a blue and white dotted cotton dress with a wide overlapping collar of white pique. She knew that it was getting a little late in the season to be wearing a dress such as this, but it was the most beautiful dress that she had ever owned. She remembered how she had agonized for two days before deciding to order it. Even on sale, the dress had cost ninety-eight cents. Then she messed around and let Ruby convince her that she needed to order an artificial leather purse with real looking grain to go with it.

"It has the new short flap that's ever so popular," Ruby teased. "They'll even put your initial on it free of charge." Next Ruby talked her into ordering a perky little white cotton hat. There went another thirty-nine cents. For several days she'd felt guilty about spending that much money on herself.

After dressing in her new attire, she stepped before the long, cracked mirror hanging on the back of the door. Willa thought she'd never looked better, that is until she looked at her feet. The fine, sensible oxfords, which Effie encouraged her to buy, just didn't match.

At half-light, it was with a great deal of excitement that she and Justin gathered the children of the Holler together and set out for town. When they were close enough to hear the voices of other children as well as the laughter from the adults, Justin let the young ones go. With a loud whoop, they broke into a run.

Rides and booths of all descriptions dotted the vacant lot. There were games to play; hot dogs, popcorn, and cotton candy to eat; and all kinds of cold drinks to wash down the food.

Willa and Justin weaved their way through the throngs of people, stopping now and then to watch as folks tried their luck at one of the games of skill.

From the other side of the grounds, Robert Vaughn also moved from booth to booth, sometimes trying his luck, but mostly waving the barkers off. The crush of people in the small space made it difficult to pick anyone out of the crowd. Before either Robert or Willa knew it, they were standing side by side.

"Hello, Mrs. Sinclair," he said softly.

Willa froze at the sound of his voice. After a moment's hesitation, she turned to acknowledge the greeting. Surprise flickered in her hazel eyes. Hanging on his arm was none other than Sara Jane Lockwood. As quickly as possible, Willa recovered and assumed a smiling expression.

Sara Jane took in Willa's appearance with a critical eye. Knowing that she outshone Willa, she preened in her beautiful mauve, three-piece suit of Canton silk crepe. A batiste blouse with a collar of embroidered eyelet completed the ensemble. Everything matched—hat, purse, and shoes. Sara Jane caught a glimpse of Willa's purse before Willa had time to put it behind her back. She saw that it was a cheap imitation of her purse. Sara Jane smiled maliciously. There was nothing artificial about the purse she carried, a point she intended to make to Willa. She held the purse up and fingered the three initials, S. J. L., so that Willa was sure to see it.

"You have on a new dress," Robert said to Willa.

"A bit out of season," Sara Jane quipped.

"That was uncalled for, Sara Jane," Robert shot back.

"Why Rob-bert!" Sara Jane pouted as she tugged on his arm to walk away. "She's only your maid." She raised her voice to make sure Willa overheard. "Why you insist on a maid from the Holler is beyond me.

From what I hear, they don't even have electricity or much of anything else down there. I'm surprised she even knows how to clean."

Willa closed her eyes, controlling an itch to pull Sara Jane's hair out by the roots. Swallowing hard, she took a deep breath and lifted her head with dignity.

"Ignore her, Willa," Jay Sky whispered as they moved off, his warm fingers encasing hers. "She's a classic, arrogant, egotistical asshole, bitch."

"To say the least," Willa added. She shook her head. "I would like to believe I'm capable of handling her kind. What do you think makes the Sara Janes of the world the way they are?"

"In Sara Jane's case, it's jealousy, Willa. You're a hell of a lot prettier than she is." He grabbed Willa by the hand, "Forget Sara Jane. I'm *fixin'* to take you for a ride on the Ferris Wheel."

"Why thank you, kind sir," Willa replied. "I'd be delighted." Neither Robert Vaughn nor Sara Jane Lockwood would dampen her spirits! But in truth, the evening had already been ruined for Willa Sinclair.

Glad that she didn't need to pretend any longer that she was having a good time, and thankful for the time alone, Willa waited in front of the post office while Justin rounded up the children. She took a deep breath and sank onto the bench.

At roughly the same time, Robert suggested to Sara Jane that it was time to leave. She gave him a coy look. It was still early so she was sure that he meant to take her for a ride in the country.

Robert had no intentions of taking her anywhere other than home. He hurried her across the carnival grounds into the street. His gait halted when he saw Willa, halted just enough so that Sara Jane noticed. Robert pretended he didn't see Willa and ushered Sara Jane into his car.

Willa watched the handsomely dressed couple climb into the fancy automobile. Feeling a twinge of envy, Willa rubbed her hand down her wrinkled dress and wondered what it would be like to be in their shoes. Having been raised on the opposite side of the fence, it seemed to Willa that the couple had it all. What would the old blue hen say? Oh yes, she thought. *They got the world by the tail on a down hill pull.* Willa instantly hated them for it.

Chapter 18
To Extract

The next Friday after an all-night delivery of a bouncing baby boy, Robert arrived home at the crack of dawn, exhausted and blurry eyed. He unfurled himself from the Speedster, took a look at his watch, and opened the back door. Dropping down into one of the kitchen chairs, he propped his elbows on the table and rubbed his hands over his face. He was tired of playing games with Willa. He had made a terrible mistake, and he thought he had figured out a way to deal with her. But now he felt that after she saw him with Sara Jane, she might…Oh, what the hell did he care anyway?

He decided he wanted a cup of coffee. He glanced around, trying to locate the coffeepot. Normally the kitchen was just a room he passed through to get outside. He had never taken the time to study its contents. His eyes narrowed in surprise as if seeing the kitchen for the first time. Willa's touch was all over the place. There was even a damn flower in the window. He gave the little plant a vicious swipe, sending it crashing to the floor. "Enough of this," he grunted, jerking his shirttail out of his pants and heading for the bedroom and a shower.

He flung his shirt across the bed and downed his trousers. With one foot in the air, he came to an abrupt halt. The house seemed unnervingly quiet, but he was certain he had heard a faint movement in the hall. His first instinct being self-preservation, he secured his pants and picked up a vase.

Slowly and seductively, Willa Sinclair, with hazel eyes wide and glowing, slithered around the doorframe into view.

He exhaled softly and set the vase down on the nearest table. His brow lifted slightly.

"I'm glad to see that you've had a change of heart," he said, reaching for her.

"Not on your life, buddy," she said and whirled just in time to avoid his arms. Without stopping, she snatched up an article from the dresser. With eyes blazing, she faced him. "Touch me and I'll smash this to kingdom come."

Robert stilled instantly, his gaze glued to the one-of-a-kind orchid enamel vanity set that had belonged to his mother. It rested in the palm of Willa's hand. His eyes darted from the vanity set to Willa's face. The malicious smile she wore assured him she was not kidding. He watched as long slim fingers reached for the delicate atomizer. Removing it from the tray, she held it out precariously over the floor. She licked her lips.

"Maybe this belongs to Sara Jane," she jeered.

A chill passed through Robert. He had to swallow hard before he was capable of speech. "No," he said softly, never taking his eyes from the set, "that doesn't belong to Sara Jane."

Willa made guttural sound. "Sara Jane or Linda Lou, what does the name matter?" she said sarcastically. "From the look on your face, I'd say it must belong to someone. I'm wondering," she said, giving the atomizer a slight jiggle in the air. "I'm wondering if you entertain all your lady friends in the same manner you entertained me." Slowly and daringly, she raised the atomizer into the air, ready to send it crashing to the floor.

"Please, don't!" he managed to say. Then in a voice that was choked and barely audible he added, "That belonged to my mother."

Willa's arm froze in mid-air. Her mouth opened and closed wordlessly. Not a sound punctuated the room for several seconds. "Oh my," she finally whispered. Ever so gently, she returned the atomizer to the tray and carefully placed it on the dresser. It was apparent to her that he was shaken by what she had almost done.

"I'm sorry," she said.

Robert didn't utter a word. For an instant, Willa saw a flicker of deep sadness in his usually cold eyes...such sadness that it made her tender heart ache. At that moment he was vulnerable, so much so that she wanted to gather him into her arms like a lost little boy. She made a slight move in his direction but stopped when she saw his expression change to anger.

Instinct told her to run. She really didn't know this man that well. He could be capable of almost anything.

"I didn't..."

"Don't!" he said coldly. "Don't say a word." He turned and walked into bathroom.

"...know," she finished in a whisper and sank to the side of the bed.

Robert stepped into the shower, letting the cold water clear his head and relax his tense body. Shortly, he emerged from the bedroom to find Willa at work. Their eyes locked for several heart-stopping seconds before a grin twitched at the corners of his mouth.

Tentatively, she returned his smile.

"Sara Jane has never been inside my house," he stated, letting his finger brush her cheek ever so lightly.

Willa stiffened. Slowly, she reached up and removed his hand from her face and took a step back. "You will never touch me again without my permission, and you will never again hurt me. Believe me, when I tell you, if you ever do, even if it means I'll rot in jail for the rest of my life, I'll kill you!"

Robert's hand drop to his side. "I never meant to hurt you the first time," he said in earnest. "Please accept my apology."

Willa's feelings still smarted, and somehow, an apology just didn't seem quite enough. "One more thing," she said. "From now on, leave my plant alone."

Chapter 19
Adultery

"What the hell was that?" Robert asked when he heard the crash. He jumped to his feet and raced to the front of the office only to find Birdie Hodges sprawled on the floor, an overturned chair by her side.

"How many times have I told you not to climb, Miss Birdie?" he admonished. He kicked the chair aside, then quickly dropped to his knees to examine her ankle. It was broken. Grabbing a roll of tape and several towels, he made a temporary splint. As gently as possible, he lifted her into his arms and carried her to the examining room.

If it had not been for the terrible nebula of pain, Birdie Hodges would have never let Robert touch her, let alone gather her body into his arms. She quickly revived when he placed his hand on her thigh and tried to remove her stocking. Having a man touch her was so offensive to the old maid that she flat out told him in no uncertain terms that she would prefer to die first.

Robert ran a hand through his thick hair in a gesture of despair. Leaning over Birdie Hodges, he looked her in the eye and said, "Since you have taken charge, tell me, how I am going to attend to you if you won't allow me to remove your clothing?"

"You'll get a woman in here, young man, and fast!" Birdie shrieked.

Since it was too early in the morning for patients, or for any of the stores to be open, Robert wondered what he should do. He glanced at the calendar. It was Friday. Willa Sinclair was not only prompt, but also an early bird. She'll be at my house, he thought, as he reached for the telephone.

In a short time, Willa entered the office.

"Quick!" Robert told her. "Help me get that damn stocking off of her!"

"You'll do no such thing," Miss Birdie informed him. "No one is touching me until you leave the room." She was a chaste woman, and he certainly wasn't going to see any more of her body than was necessary, not if she was ever going to be able to look him in the eye again. It was going to be all she could do to reveal the blue-veined leg to anyone, much less a man. By the time Robert was admitted to the room, Birdie Hodges lay trussed to the hilt in a white sheet. He couldn't help but notice the mirth that danced in Willa's eyes.

After attending to Miss Birdie's ankle, he and Willa took her home. She was left in the capable hands of her old maid sister.

Driving back to the office, Robert said, "I suspect it's going to be some time before Miss Birdie can do anymore than give orders." He hesitated for a moment, then in a crisp, impersonal voice, he added, "I'll be needing someone to help her." He faced her, looking as innocent as a child. "I'm offering you full time work, at least for a while, and with no strings attached. Are you interested?"

"I'm interested."

In no time at all, Willa learned just how much of a tyrant Miss Birdie could be. Within two days she was back in the office giving orders like a drill sergeant. Nothing that Willa did suited the old nurse. Several times during that first week, Willa wished Birdie Hodges had broken her jaw, instead of her ankle.

After several days of not feeling up to snuff, Miss Birdie, encouraged by Robert, decided to go home early. Hesitant about leaving Willa unsupervised to do the clean up, Birdie paused at the side door and for the second time, gave Willa explicit instructions. She hobbled through the door then turned and hobbled back, sticking her crutch inside the door before Willa could close it.

"Remember," she said for the third time "be sure you sterilize everything, including the glass containers before you refill them with tongue depressors and cotton balls."

Willa had visions of Miss Birdie with a mouth full of cotton balls. A few seconds after Miss Birdie disappeared, Willa peaked around the door to make sure she was really gone. Breathing a sigh of relief, she closed the door. "Thank goodness," she muttered.

"Mrs. Sinclair?"

The mere sound of his voice set her heart to pounding. Breathing deeply, she placed the container of cotton balls aside and entered the examining room.

Rinsing his hands at the sink, Robert addressed her in a sympathetic tone, "Don't let the Old Bird get you down."

Willa moved around him to the small table adjacent to the sink. Raising her eyebrows, she asked, "The old bird?"

Robert laughed. "That's my pet name for her. But don't you dare tell on me," he cautioned.

Willa smiled and reached for the basket of utensils.

Robert, in turn, reached for a towel hanging over the basket. When their fingers accidentally touched, they both jerked away as if they had burned each other.

"Well, what do you know," he said as lightly as possible. "I touched you and I'm still living." His eyes caught hers and held them with a flaming intensity. "Whatever happens from here on out is up to you," he said softly.

Willa hadn't expected this, and she was stunned by it. She closed her eyes. The time had come to either accept her fate or run from it as fast as she possibly could. As Effie would put it, "It's time to shit or get off the pot." She took a deep breath. Why did she have to think of Mama at this most inappropriate time? She knew that was not all that Mama would say, if she only knew, but she didn't want to think about her now.

Reaching a decision, Willa took one almighty step toward Robert Vaughn. Placing her hands on his chest, she seductively let her fingers trail upward over his shoulders and around his neck. Drawing his lips down to meet hers, she whispered, "I believe it would be a good idea if you were to lock the front door."

"Are you sure?"

"Oh, I'm sure," she said before biting his ear.

Triumphantly, he led her into his inner office. Without saying a single word, he lifted her onto the edge of the desk.

Certain that this time she was in control, Willa Sinclair did the unthinkable; she spread her legs to welcome him.

Chapter 20
From the Wrongdoing

As the icy fist of fear clutched her heart, Willa Sinclair collapsed onto the bed and waited for the paralyzing nausea to lessen its hold on her. She closed her eyes and hung on to the side of the bed, struggling to draw air into her lungs and, at the same time, desperately trying to stifle the rise of burning liquid in her throat. Once the feeling subsided and she could breathe easily again, the finality of her situation stabbed at her like an attacker with a sharp knife. She was pregnant.

Willa buried her hands deep into her thick hair, clutching huge handfuls tightly in her fists. She rolled her head from side to side, pulling until she shed tears of pain. Listlessly, she managed to sit up and pull her sweat-soaked gown over her head. Tossing the gown to the floor, she arose from the bed, staggered to the dry sink and pulled the wash-pan from the wall, filled it with cool water, and bathed her burning face. It took firm resolution for her to gather the energy to dress herself. When she finished, she dropped onto the chair in front of the dresser and once again came face to face with a pale Willa Sinclair. The natural shading that normally drew one's attention to her hazel eyes now made them look like two burned holes in a blanket. She made a half-hearted attempt to untangle her hair. In frustration she let the brush drop to her lap. Unable to face the image in the mirror, she picked up the towel and threw it over the mirror.

"This pile of shit I live in just keeps on getting deeper," she moaned. In desperation, she bowed her head and called on the Almighty, "Lord, have mercy on me. Would you mind if I talk to someone a little closer to home about this one?"

It was just before sunrise and the Holler was awakening. Soon the air would be thick with the smell of coffee perking and meat frying. Any other time, Willa would have welcomed the smell. Now her stomach churned at the mere suggestion of food. Nevertheless, out of routine, she made herself a cup of coffee, opened the back door, and sat on the steps, trying to sort out her grief and misery in private. She thought about confiding in Ruby. Ruby would understand, but then it was Jay Sky whom she had always trusted with her secrets.

The whiskey-still was in operation, and she soon heard the voices of the men gathering to cross the ditches. Willa watched as Pebo lumbered up the path to take his position at the edge of the Holler. She heard Bean bark, then light out after a rabbit. Closing her eyes, she dropped her chin to her chest. Guilt washed over her, she was envying Pebo his simple Peter Pan way of life.

Above all the usual noises of the Holler, she could hear Papa cursing John for the mess he had made during the night when he had fallen over the woodpile, scattering the kindling that Ben had so neatly stacked the day before.

Willa drew her knees under her chin and watched in silence until she could see the sunlight dancing through the leaves of the trees on the far side of the river. She sighed, gave herself a mental shake, rose and entered the house to wake, feed, and bathe Aster. By sheer force of will, she managed to complete her morning chores before carrying Aster to Effie's house. She took a deep breath and went in search of Jay Sky.

Justin Rider docked his boat, climbed the bank, and perched himself on a stump beside the communal table under the cottonwood tree. He placed a bucket between his long legs and set about cleaning his early morning catch. He paused for a second when he noticed Willa approaching. Her comportment told him she was not seeking him out to discuss the weather. In fact it had been a while since Willa had sought him out at all.

"Have you got a minute to talk?" she asked.

Jay Sky smiled, showing his perfect white teeth. "As Grandfather would say, my ears are open."

Taking a deep breath, Willa pulled up one of the crude benches to the communal table and joined him.

Justin kept at his work, but he listened carefully to every word Willa uttered. She told him about her affair with Robert, not sparing herself in the least. Willa knew that Jay Sky didn't care for Robert. She wanted him to understand that *she* was just as responsible as Robert was for turning what had transpired into an affair. She wanted Jay Sky to understand. As she spoke, she desperately tried to convey her loneliness, her desire to love and to be loved. Then she told him she was pregnant.

Jay Sky was slow in responding. She knew he seldom showed feeling, but it seemed his response was more non-committal than usual. She felt awkward, and a little embarrassed. Looking across the river, she studiously examined the early morning mist that had gathered over the water. "Are you disappointed in me?" she asked, and then gave a nervous laugh. "That's a stupid question. Even I'm disappointed in me."

"Look at me," Justin said. "Do I look disappointed?"

"Since when were you easy to read?" she said dryly. Leaning forward, she placed her elbows on the table and breathed a tiny sigh of relief that she had finally shared her problem. "You're too much like Grandfather Will Sky, for that. I remember when we'd get into trouble as kids, I'd see the same look in his face that I see in yours." Willa raised her brows,

"Now that I think about it, I think he enjoyed making us squirm until he announced our punishment."

Justin laughed. "I think you're right."

"You're so like him, Jay Sky," Willa said softly.

Justin picked up the catfish he was skinning and walked to the hand pump. Squatting down, he rinsed the fish, then his hands.

Willa could see the muscles ripple in his long arms and shoulders as he pulled himself to his feet. The clothes he wore were old and faded, but they still enhanced his dark hair and coppery complexion. She could easily see why Ruby was so in love with him. She couldn't think of better words to describe him other than to say that Jay Sky Rider was as beautiful as a man could be both inside and out.

Justin studied Willa out of the corner of his eye. He had given much thought in recent months as to how he should react were she to confide in him, especially if it was about Robert. He swallowed the strong urge to admonish her for getting mixed up with Vaughn in the first place. Willa had always dreamed too much, but he couldn't fault her for that. He knew that anyone forced to live in the Holler had nothing but dreams. He placed the fish on the worktable and began to fillet it.

Willa's eyes followed his every move. "You don't seem very surprised, and you don't need to tell me. I know you're disappointed in me."

"I would never presume to judge you, Willa, nor am I surprised. I've known about you and Vaughn for a long time."

"You're kidding me," she said in a small voice. "I didn't think anyone knew."

"You forget how well I know you." He paused and gave her a look that conveyed the depth of compassion he was feeling for her. "I've been afraid for you, honey, afraid from the beginning that you'd get hurt."

Willa toyed with the sleeve of her dress. "When did you first know?"

"I had strong suspicions when you began to work on your vocabulary. I knew for certain the night we took in the carnival."

"You think working on my vocabulary is a dumb thing to do, don't you?" She could feel the flush creeping into her cheeks. She felt so foolish that she kept her eyes trained on the fish that he was expertly filleting.

"No, not at all," he answered quickly, sensing her discomfort. "That's the right thing to do. It's just the reason you've chosen for doing it. It won't change anything. You'll still be who you are, and he'll still be who he is." Justin stopped what he was doing, laid his work aside, and strode around the table. Squatting in front of her, he took his thumb and lifted her face so that he could look her straight in the eyes. Willa breathed in the smell of him. Except for his hands, she thought, he smells so clean, refreshing, like the outdoors.

"You know, honey, it's not that you aren't good enough for him. In my opinion, you're too good. I'm just afraid the only thing you can possibly get out of this is heartbreak." Rising, he washed his hands, dried them on his pants, and then jammed his hands in his pockets. Pacing back and forth in front of her, he diligently searched his brain for the right words. The last thing he wanted to do was to add to her hurt, but there was no easy way to say what he needed.

At long last, he stopped, bent down again, and took her hands into his. Squeezing them, he said, "You'll never be able to hold him here, nor go with him when he decides to leave. He's from another world, one that's born and bred into him, Willa, same as the river is born and bred into us." Then he grimaced at the harshness of his word.

With tears streaming down her face, Willa managed a slight nod of her head before burying her face in her hands.

Justin dug in his back pocket for his handkerchief, handed it to her, then waited patiently until she had recovered enough to resume the conversation.

Wiping her eyes, Willa sucked in a deep breath. "I know, I know, Jay Sky, but I can't seem to stop myself. My mind tells me one thing, and my heart and body tell me another." She gave a shaky little laugh. Rising from the bench, Willa kissed Jay Sky on the cheek. "You're a good friend, and I thank you for it."

"I'm sorry I can't do more to help," he said, then his eyes took on a twinkle. "I could beat him up, make him suffer. I won't deny that I would probably enjoy it."

Willa shook her head.

"Not even a tiny knot on the head?" he persisted.

"No," she said, standing up, and brushing the debris from her skirt. Taking a few steps in the direction of home, she paused. When she turned and faced him, Justin caught a slight glint in her hazel eyes. A soft smile touched the corners of her lovely mouth as a hint of the old Willa returned. "So you think I'm being a bit presumptuous?"

"Oh presumptuous, is it? No-oo, I don't think you are being presumptuous...maybe, I think you should be a bit more astute from now on."

"Astute," she repeated and gave him a wink. Since it was not a word anyone had much use for in the Holler, Willa wasn't sure of its meaning. It wouldn't take her long to find out. She was the proud owner of a brand new Webster's Dictionary.

Chapter 21
Self-Denial

Without warning, the dreams of abandonment that had haunted him off and on since childhood returned, and then began to change. Robert Vaughn sat on the edge of the bed, holding his head in his hands. With a deep sigh, he crawled under the covers and closed his eyes. He was bone tired and knew he must sleep. As he suspected, in a few hours the dreams prodded him awake. Unable to stop himself, he gathered the pillow into his arms and buried his face into the softness. Breathing in, he savored her lingering scent. It was always this way after they made love.

"Make love," the voice in his head scoffed.

Robert scoffed in return and was ready to vocalize a response when he caught himself. Fearing for his sanity, he sat up on the side of the bed and raised his hands in a gesture of helplessness. "Damn!" he said. Then his eyes settled on the glass of stale whiskey. Hoping to dispel the voice and the dark cloud of gloom that hung over him, he picked it up and downed it in one swallow.

Thirty minutes later, he was sitting at the desk in his office, trying without success to concentrate on the work before him. He shoved the work aside and slung the pencil across the room. Lowering his face to his hands, he told himself that he might as well face it. He knew her body as well as he knew his own. Willa was pregnant. In his heart, he knew that he should speak to her about it. The more he tried to think of what he might say, the more the old familiar terror swelled within his brain.

"No!" the voice thundered. "That would be getting too close." He clinched his fists and did something he had not done since he was a boy. He struggled to bring forth that part of him that he knew would deal with this problem. So powerful was the effort that his fingernails cut his flesh, but he felt no pain. By the time the metamorphosis was complet-ed, his palms were stained with blood. Taking a deep breath to relax, he flexed his shoulders, and let his head roll from side to side.

"Why," part of him demanded, "should you discuss her pregnancy with her? She has a husband. That is, unless she makes an issue of her condition."

Willa would never make an issue of it, Robert knew, but someone lurking in the shadows soon might.

Five months into Willa's pregnancy, Robert had a visitor. John Sinclair, permeating the air with a sharp aroma of a still, sauntered into the doctor's office. With affected dignity, he said, "I ain't a man to shilly-shally, Doc, so I'll get right to the point. It appears to me you done knocked up my wife."

Robert jumped up from the desk and towered over John. "Get the hell out of my office, Sinclair, before I throw you out!" he hissed.

John scurried for the door. "Whatever you say, Doc, whatever you say. You don't have to get riled. I'm jest tryin' to have a little man-to-man talk with ye. Thought you might be willin' ta help me out…but then if you ain't willin…" his voice became menacing, "I just see that *she* pays me to keep my mouth shut. It don't make no never mine to me."

Robert caught the door before John could close it and motioned him back into the room.

Feeling his power over the situation increasing, John dropped into the chair in front of the desk, conjuring up a hurt expression. "The way I see it, Doc, I'm the injured party here and you owe me something."

Robert held up his hand. "Cut the dramatics, Sinclair, and get to the point."

Dropping all pretenses, John sneered. "I guess what you want to hear is that I don't give a damn how many brats you have with her, and that's a fact." John's eyes narrowed as hate spread across his face. "Since you ask, there's a second verse to this song, Doc, ever one you have is gonna cost, if not you, *her* just a little bit more."

"So this is blackmail is it?

John shrugged. "Call it anyway you see it."

"What's it going to take, Sinclair?"

"Just a few dollars a week, Doc, that's all."

Robert's eyes narrowed as he studied John for several long seconds. "If I agree to this, do I have your word, such as it is, not to approach Mrs. Sinclair?"

"Absolutely, ab-so-lute-ly!" John Sinclair groveled. But John, lacking scruples, had other plans. When he left the doctor's office, he headed home.

The next item on his agenda was to threaten Willa in order to get his bed moved back into the shack.

Chapter 22
Illegitimate Child

The elements lashed at southeast Missouri with a relentless fury for over two weeks. Ben Melton, Justin Rider, and the twins stood on the bank staring at the churning water of the river.

"It won't be long now, men," Ben yelled as best he could between coughing and sneezing. "If something don't give, and it don't look like she's gonna, we best start packin' up and gettin' ready to head for high ground."

Justin gave Ben a look of concern. "First off, you better get in out of this weather, Ben," he admonished.

Ben nodded. "Sure as hell ain't no time to be sick," he said as he turned to go. Despite how bad Ben felt, he had to take a few minutes to check on Willa. He tapped on the door, opened it, and walked into the kitchen. His heart went out to her when he found her sitting listlessly at the kitchen table. He wished to the Good Lord that he knew how to help her. At the moment, he wasn't in any condition to even help himself.

The glazed, fevered look in Ben's eyes momentarily jarred Willa from the apathy.

"Papa! What are you doing out in this weather? You're sick!" she declared. "You should be in bed."

"Now, Hon, I feel bad enough without you adding to it." Ben rubbed his aching shoulders. "Anyway, I'm on my way home. I just wanted to stop by long enough to see how you're doing?"

She reached for a bowl. "I'm doing fine, Papa," she said, trying to sound cheerier. Pulling a bench out for Ben, she said. "Why don't you sit down here and have some soup?"

Pain sliced through Ben's head. Closing his eyes, he gave a low moan. "Thank you for the offer, but I don't think I could eat a bite of anything just now."

Rather than accept the refusal, Willa filled a Mason jar with soup. "Take this with you, Papa, and promise me you'll try to drink some of the broth."

"I promise," Ben said, though he doubted he could.

Willa watched him go, tears filling her eyes. "Take care, Papa," she whispered. What in heaven's name would she ever do without him?

Ben, racked with chills and fever, headed back to his shack where he undressed and crawled into bed. "Effie," he said wearily, "we ain't talked about it, but you know that baby Willa's carryin' ain't John's."

"I know," Effie whispered.

"What do you think our girl will do now?" he asked.

Effie tucked him in with a hot water bottle, searching her mind for a maxim to fit the situation. When she couldn't come up with one, she shook her head in despair.

Meanwhile in her kitchen, Willa took the bowl she had offered Ben and filled it with the steaming soup. After several bites, she found that she too had no appetite. Dropping the spoon into the bowl, she gave it a vicious shove, spilling the contents onto the table.

For most of that morning, Willa had done little but sit hopelessly at the table, reflecting on the events that led up to her pregnancy. Over and over she played them, like a broken record on Ruby's Victoria. She sniffed, blew her nose, and surveyed the kitchen, letting her red-rimmed eyes bring into focus the flimsy walls, cold floors, rattling windows, and straw-filled mattresses. No matter how hard she tried, no matter how many times she scrubbed it, no matter how many flour sack curtains she made, she still lived in an ugly shack.

Pride had kept Willa from going to Robert with her pregnancy. Instead she sought out Maw NanEmmer's help.

"You ain't got nothin' ta fear," Maw told her. "I reckon I've delivered more babies in my time than any doctor ever thought about deliverin'. I 'speck you have another week to go," Maw had said that very afternoon.

Willa glanced down at her protruding stomach. Some revenge! I really made him pay, didn't I? At last, she gave up the dreary pretense, put her head down on her arms and wept.

Despite Ben's scoffing, a part of Effie Melton clung to the Indian ways. She believed that evil spirits haunted the darkness. Preparing herself for the dangers of the night ahead, she banked the fire and listened to the haunting sound of the pounding rain. Reflecting on Ben's unanswered question, she suddenly blurted out, "Play with fire and you get burnt," but Ben was far too sick to hear her.

Unable to sleep, Willa knew that she could vouch for every rumble of thunder and every strike of lightening that pierced the sky. By three in the morning, she was weary enough to be convinced that the pain dancing up and down her spine was part of her punishment. Why else would it take such glee in causing her to echo the groans of the shack, violently whipped by the wind and rain. We are both begging for mercy, she thought.

Gradually, her tired mind floated into the crepuscular light of sleep where one never quite gives up consciousness. It was in this state of delirium that she fancied she heard someone calling her name. "I'm coming," she heard herself say. She rolled onto her back, rubbed the sleep from her eyes, and listened. A ripple of fear ran down her spine.

She had been so immersed in her own misery that she had completely forgotten about the ditches.

"Omigod!" she said, jumping from the bed and opening the kitchen door, only to find the muddy water of the river winding itself around the shack like a giant brown snake. She threw on her robe and hurried onto the porch. Though the morning was misty, she could see Justin rowing toward her in a boat.

"It's getting bad; better get ready to move out," Justin called to her. Glancing at Willa's protruding stomach, he added. "Is John home?"

"He's here. Jay Sky, would you do me a favor and go check on Papa?"

"I already have, Willa. He's pretty sick. I'm on my way to get them out now. Do you think you can depend on John to get you and Aster to dry land?"

"Don't worry about me; you just take care of Papa."

"I'll leave you a boat," he said, reluctantly. Justin did not like the idea of leaving her in John's hands. But at the moment, he had no choice.

"Thanks," Willa said as pain shot through her back, causing her to grab the door for support. She turned her head so that Justin couldn't see the pain in her face. Giving him a final wave, she hurried back inside. As quickly as her condition would allow, she gathered together a few necessities to move out.

"John!" she shouted over and over until finally she penetrated his stupor. "The water is coming up! We've got to get out of the Holler!" She hurried across the wet soggy floor into the kitchen to pack a few utensils. The pain in her lower back was increasing. "Oh, dear Lord, don't let it be now," she prayed. Straightening up with a groan, she continued to urge John into action. "Papa says we're in for the worst high water we've seen yet."

John sat on the side of the bed and glared at Willa, "Papa says, Papa says," he mimicked. Ignoring the obvious pain on her face, he turned back and reached for his shoes. "You think that yore old man knows ever-thing," he said, with his usual nasal twang.

Willa heaved a sigh—same song, second verse, she thought. "I have never said that Papa knows everything, John, but he definitely knows about high water." The next pain brought tears to her anguished face.

"Never mind that now, John. I need you to help me pack. Papa is sick and not able to help us, so it's up to you to get us out of here." Willa closed her eyes and took a deep breath.

"Keep calm," she whispered. "Please, John, for one time in your life, listen to me. We're in danger." She wiped the tears from her eyes with both hands. "I fear that Papa has pneumonia. I'm afraid Aster has it too. And the water is getting higher and higher, and I'm afraid that I'm about to have the baby."

Grabbing his hat and rain slicker, John headed for the door.

"Where are you going?" Willa demanded.

"To town," he said. "To find a damn dry place."

"You can't go off and leave us here. Please, John," she begged. "Listen to reason, there won't be time enough for..."

But John didn't listen. Instead, he slammed the door in her face. Willa heard the lid to the wood box open and close, then she heard him cursing a rat that had taken refuge on the small front porch.

"Oh Lord," she moaned, "he has a bottle. Lord, let him make it to town before he gets too drunk to remember what he's doing." She frantically surveyed the room. How many rats, she wondered, have already gotten inside the house? I've got to get hold of myself. "Focus, Willa, focus," she breathed.

Justin settled Ben and Effie as quickly as possible. Concern for Willa had plagued him since the moment he left her. He had to get back to the Holler to make sure she and Aster were safe. Halfway there, he met John drunk and stumbling along the road.

"You drunken idiot," he said, "you can't even stay sober long enough to take care of your family." At the edge of the Holler, Justin leaped into his boat and paddled as swiftly as possible through the rising waters to

Willa's shack. He tried forcing the front door open, but found that it was swollen too tightly to budge. Without a choice, he took an axe from the woodbox and chopped the door down.

Willa, standing in ankle deep water and clutching a cotton hoe in her hand, gave a sigh of relief. "I knew you would come," she said as she fended off several rats that were desperately trying to take refuge on the bed in which a semi-conscious Aster lay.

It was the granddaddy of all floods for southeast Missouri. It rained day and night, sending more than 300 folks from the low-lying areas to seek shelter. The floodwater continued to rise for several days, forcing more and more people to seek refuge. Eventually boxcars had to be brought in by the railroad for housing.

Newspapers as far as St. Louis were filled with stories of strife and hardship. One article in the Daily Dunklin Democrat read...*Dr. Wheeler Davis, Dunklin County health physician...announced that he made a visit to the flooded area around Hornersville on Wednesday of this week. He found the conditions among the refugees to be the worst of any community in the county. He reports that 29 patients suffering from pneumonia, influenza, or typhoid are being housed in an emergency hospital located in the basement of the Methodist Church at Hornersville. Dr. Robert Vaughn, along with several other doctors in the area, have been working tirelessly both day and night caring for the afflicted.*

Willa, Aster, and Ben were among those in the makeshift hospital. Upon admittance, Ben and little Aster were diagnosed with pneumonia. Willa was in the final stages of labor.

Gensi Sinclair entered the world amidst the turmoil. The nurses at the makeshift hospital tended three-year old Aster night and day, until her fever broke. Thinking the weakened little girl would sleep through the night, they placed her on a cot near her mother. In the wee hours of the morning, Aster crawled into Willa's bed only to find a tiny, wrinkled bundle sharing her place.

"What you do, Mommy?" she asked.

"I got you a baby sister, Honey. Would you like to see her?" Willa lifted the cotton blanket so that Aster could view the tiny face.

"My baby," Aster stated.

Willa cradled Aster in one arm and the newborn in the other. "I'm thinking about naming her Genevieve, Aster. How do you like it?"

"Gensi," three-year old Aster stated.

Willa stroked Aster's head. "If that's what you want to call her, Gensi it is."

Willa kissed them both and cried. She felt so guilty. The worst of her guilt stemmed from the fact that her two girls only had her to rely upon, and at the moment, she was totally inadequate.

Several weeks after Gensi's birth, Willa Sinclair walked into Robert's office. Leaning on his desk, she took a deep breath and announced in no uncertain terms, "I'm here for one reason and one reason alone. As of Monday morning, I will be returning to work. I'm asking you to extend my hours to full time and to raise my wages to equal Miss Birdie's since I have assumed the majority of her duties."

As hard as he tried, Robert could not bring himself to meet Willa's eyes. "Money is no problem, Mrs. Sinclair; you know that. I've always been willing to pay you." As he shuffled the papers about on his desk, he asked, "How much do you want?"

"I believe I just stated my terms." Pulling herself to her full height, she continued, "there is one other thing that I would like to make perfectly clear. There are no…fringe benefits attached to this arrangement in any form or fashion."

"Damn!" she thought as she headed home. Jay Sky might not approve of her decision to return to work, but if he could have heard her speech, she knew in her heart that he would have been proud.

Chapter 23
Family

More and more often, Willa found herself very short of temper because of her husband's lack of contribution to the family's well being. She rounded the corner of the house to find nine-year old Aster digging and scratching in the dirt next to the old shed where John had once slept.

"Get out of that dirt, Aster Sinclair!"

Aster grabbed her fruit jar and scurried to obey.

Willa entered through the back door of the house, knowing she had spoken too sharply to her eldest daughter. If she had stopped to think, instead of just lashing out, she would have realized that Aster was only digging red worms to go fishing with Jay Sky and Pebo.

Willa took a deep breath, ran her hand down her face, and huffed the air from her lungs. As hard as she tried, she was not able to control the anger that welled up inside of her.

"Don't take it out on the girls!" she told herself in frustration. "None of the mess you've made of your life is your children's fault." On days like this, Willa realized with a cold clarity just how obsessed with Robert Vaughn she had become. Although for over six year, she had rebuffed Robert's many attempts to resume their intimacy, he still remained her breath of life—even to the point of sometimes neglecting the girls. Having Ben and Effie to look after them made it too easy. She tried to soothe her conscience by telling herself that she earned enough not only to raise the girls, but to help her parents as well.

Taking her apron and wiping the perspiration from her face, she watched Aster run around the corner of the shack, more than likely looking for Gensi.

"Damn you, John!" she thought to herself. "I should've known better than to mention work in front of you."

Cutting wood was grueling work enough for a young man, let alone someone Ben's age. Since it was Saturday morning, no one was available to help him but Jay Sky, and she'd be damned if she was going to ask him and have him break off his promised fishing trip with her girls.

"When are you going to realize, Papa," Willa said aloud, "that you're getting too old for this? Sometimes you can be downright impossible," she grumbled. "I begged you, Papa, let me buy some coal this year, but oh no, you gotta cut wood," she said sarcastically.

Aster knew the warning signs. Mama was madder'n hell. She raced across the yard, stopping only long enough to deposit the jar of fishing worms under the corner of the house.

"Lazy damn old some-of-britches has run off somewhere agin'," Aster muttered. "Just so's he won't have ta cut wood." Those were the very words she heard Papa say to Granny that morning. She wondered what a "some-of-britches" was anyway. You said it when you got mad, she guessed, 'cause when Papa got mad, he said it a lot!

Making a mad dash for the old cypress tree in the front of the house, Aster mimicked Willa. "Gensi!" She yelled, "git out'a that tree!"

Gensi raised her tiny blonde head and peered over the cypress knees where she lay, curled up on a piece of an old quilt. This was her favorite place for making up stories.

"Come on, Gensi, Jay Sky and Pebo's ready to go fishin'."

Gensi jumped to her feet. "Fishin'," she declared. How could she have forgotten? She loved to go fishin', especially with Jay Sky. He was her bestest friend in the whole wide world. "Jay Sky got us a fishin' pole?" Gensi questioned as she ran to keep up with Aster.

"Hell yes, Gensi. You know he's got us a fishin' pole. How we gonna fish without one?" The tone of Aster's answer was patronizing.

"Looky at my worms, Pebo! Damn good fat ones too, don't you think?" Aster yelled as the two little girls ran up the ditch dump.

Pebo took the jar in his hand and studied the worms for several seconds. He nodded his head in agreement. "Good as I ever seed."

Willa watched Justin make his way up the bank from the water's edge, carrying two small fishing poles and two wild turkey feathers. He approached Pebo and the girls.

Aster held up the fruit jar full of dirt and worms. "Looky, Jay Sky, look at my da—uh…fat worms."

"Mine too!" Gensi chimed in, jumping up and down.

Exasperated with Gensi, Aster forgot the promise she had made to Jay Sky not to use swear words. "Hell, Gensi, I dug em!"

Justin admonished Aster with his dark sooty eyes. "But, we will share, won't we, Foul Mouth?" he said in a stern voice.

Aster gave him a contrite look and nodded her head.

"That's better," he said and immediately gave the girls a warm gentle smile, showing strong white teeth in a chiseled face.

Justin made a production of pinning the turkey feathers in the girls' hair. Then he addressed them by the Indian names he had given them. Foul Mouth fit Aster perfectly, considering the language she used.

"I bet you girls can out fish me and the Chief today," he said, pointing to Pebo, who sported a feather of his own, which hung precariously over one ear.

Justin turned to Gensi. He deepened his voice and puffed out his chest. "What is your name, oh fair Indian maiden?"

Gensi made a curtsy. "My name is Eyes of Grass, Brave Sky Rider."

"Well, Eyes of Grass, do you want to ride for a while or do you feel like walking?"

"Ride, ride," she gleefully shouted.

Justin lifted Gensi's slender frame to his shoulders and strolled effortlessly down the riverbank, all the while whistling a merry tune.

Pebo and Aster brought up the rear, deep in a discussion about damn fat worms and how many fish they were sure to catch.

Willa watched until they disappeared. She mentally shook herself out of her preoccupation. She knew she needed to hurry if she was going to head off Ben before he went to cut the wood. He still considered wimin's work to be wimin's work and men's work to be men's work, and if he could, she knew that he would try to outsmart her.

As quickly as possible, she changed into a tattered pair of overalls and a long-sleeved shirt. If only John would do some work, she thought as she balled her long thick hair onto the top of her head. She shook her head in disgust. When was she going to learn that John was just as Effie said, useless as tits on a boor hog.

Ben walked around the corner of the shack with the crosscut saw on one shoulder and a hand axe on the other. He saw Willa sitting on the steps and knew what she was up to.

"Don't reckon that sonofabitch has showed up yet."

"You know he hasn't, Papa," Willa answered. "Papa, I'm going to ask you again to let me buy a load of coal. And for heaven sakes, why won't you let me buy Mama an oil-burning cook stove?"

"Cause yore mama don't want one, and as for the coal, I've always cut my wood, and I still ain't too old to do it."

"That's a matter of opinion," Willa grumbled. She got up off the steps and took the axe from Ben's hand. "Then let's go."

"You ain't going with me, girl."

"Try and stop me."

Ben Melton, in his no nonsense manner, propped his foot on the steps and asked for at least the thousandth time, "Why don't you run John's ass off, Hon? He ain't no good."

"I don't know why, Papa," she lied.

"Think about it, you been supportin' him now for all these years and just makin' life easy for him."

"I know, Papa, I know." Privately, she thought of Gensi and what would happen if she were to kick him out.

It was a losing argument and Ben knew it. Ben shook his head in disgust and headed for the river. He loved his daughter dearly. For the life of him, he didn't know how to save her. He studied her while they prepared the boat to cross the river, wondering how she endured and still retained a beauty that he considered beyond compare.

Ben sighed and glanced up at the sun. For Willa's sake, they'd cut mostly light stuff close to the riverbank. "We won't go far today," he told her after she expertly shoved the boat off the bank and jumped in as ably as any man could.

Ben steered the boat toward the opposite bank. "I think we'll cut along the bank yonder," he said, pointing in the southeast direction with the paddle.

As they worked, Ben kept glancing at Willa. He knew a little about her relationship with the doctor, at least as much as he wanted to know. He vowed a long time ago to stay out of it, but he couldn't help but wonder if there would ever be any happiness for his lovely will-o'-the-wisp.

After three trips across the river, Ben finally placed his hands on his aching back and stretched. "I think that will be enough to hold Mama for a while, don't you? I'll get Pebo to help me haul the stack to the house in the morning, so why don't you run along and get cleaned up?"

Willa smiled. It was the first smile Ben had seen on her face all day.

As soon as Willa entered the back door of the shack, she ripped off the shirt and overalls, grabbed a towel along with her threadbare wrapper, and headed out back to enjoy the simple luxury of the shower that Ben had rigged up for her.

She pulled the plug from the oil drum and gave a sigh of pure pleasure as the water cascaded over her weary body. When the drum was empty, Willa wrapped her hair in the towel, threw on the wrapper, and stepped out of the tiny enclosure. With eyes fixed on the ground, she rounded the corner and ran headlong into the arms of Robert Vaughn.

The sudden impact of their bodies sent the towel to the ground. The sweet-scented mass of hair tumbled about her face.

Robert's eyes fixed on a bead of moisture that dripped from the end of a curl then slowly trickled down her neck toward the inadequate covering on her breast. Carefully, he secured the droplet on the ball of his right thumb, then ever so gently, he massaged the areola through the damp wrapper. He felt the tip enlarge and grow taut beneath his thumb.

Despite the rigid control Willa practiced, her body tingled, sending her a distinct message.

Without a word, Robert dropped his hand to his side, stepped back, and walked away—looking as if he had slept in his clothes.

Willa took a deep breath, inhaling the infusion into her lungs as powerful as an addictive drug. As she watched him go, she realized that she had never seen him before without his scrupulous grooming. He looks so weary, she thought. She closed her eyes and knew that she too was growing weary of it all. Why, she asked herself, after all these years, did she have this driving need to punish him, or was it a driving need to punish herself?

"Dear God," she said. "I honestly don't know anymore."

Chapter 24
Friend

Six-year old Gensi sat on the side of the bed struggling with her shoelaces. Her mama had told Aster that from now on she could not tie Gensi's shoes. Since mama's not at home, Gensi thought, she knew that she could cry until Aster did it for her 'cause Granny Melton had said that she was born with her bladder in her eye. But, on second thought, crying would take too much effort, so she tied the laces into knots. Giving them a final pat, she jumped off the bed.

"You wanna go play?" she asked her sister.

"Naw," Aster answered, giving Gensi a shy look out of the corner of her eye. She thought it best not to tell her little sister about her plans to go up the path to play with her newest best friend, Dessie.

Gensi got down on her hands and knees and searched under the bed, trying to locate her jump rope. She finally found it in a box of old stuff right where Mama said it was supposed to go. When she got to her feet, she sniffed the air. Every time she got close to Aster, something burned her nose. Climbing into the rocking chair by the heating stove, she rocked and eyed her sister for several moments. Something didn't seem quite right about the way she looked. For some reason, Aster was purposely keeping her back turned. Gensi stopped rocking and decided she needed to make a closer inspection of her sister.

Gensi's eyes sparkled with mischief as she circled Aster. Finally, Aster gave up, and Gensi got a look at her hair. In an attempt to pin curl her bangs, Aster had frizzled them all across her forehead. Gensi said, "Your hair looks like a stump full of granddaddies with their legs stickin' up in the air. You know what Granny says when you do your bangs like that. If Granny was here, she'd make you wet'em and comb'em out."

Gensi sniffed the air again and wrinkled her nose at the smell. All of a sudden she remembered Aster's promise from last Saturday—that they'd each spend their dime on candy. "Then we'll play house," she had announced. "You be the mama, and I'll be the baby. You feed me your candy, and then you can be the baby, and I'll feed you my candy."

Gensi had loved the game. Since ordinarily Aster *never* let her be the mama when they played house, she had readily agreed. Regrettably, when her candy was all gone, Aster stopped playing. Later she found out that Aster had secretly spent her dime for a bottle of *Ben Hur* perfume at Burn's Five and Ten Cent store. So she had been tricked again! She thought she deserved to try some of the perfume, but Aster wouldn't let her, so she made fun of her sister.

"EE—uuck, you stink!" Her eyes dropped to Aster's chest. "You ain't got any…titties."

"I do too," Aster shot back.

"You didn't have any yester'dy and 'sides, they all lumpy, and titties ain't suppose to be lumpy. I'm gonna tell Granny! **Grannnnn—eeee.**"

"Okay, okay" Aster conceded. She turned her back to Gensi, reached down the front of her dress and brought out two fistfuls of wadded-up newspaper which she conceded to herself had been scratchin' her chest anyway.

I got even with her, Gensi crowed to herself. She ran into the yard with her jumping rope.

"Saniflush, saniflush," she chanted. Her foot caught in the rope, causing her to miss. She started all over again.

"Saniflush, saniflush, cleans your teeth without a brush," she sang out. She missed again and just kept on missing. Finally she gave up jumping rope all together, threw the rope under the house, and wandered around in the front yard. She was more intent on keeping her eyes trained on the house so that Aster couldn't slip out without her knowing about it. Last Saturday she'd fooled her and went off without her, but this time she had it all figured out. She knew Aster was going to try to trick her and go up to Dessie Pate's house again today and she'd be ready.

Finally, Aster ran out the door and across the yard, leaving a trail of cheap perfume behind her.

"Can I go?" Gensi called after her.

"Naw, you cain't go. Dessie don't like you. You're too little to play with us. 'Sides," Aster called as she ran up the path, "Dessie's gonna teach me how to do the jitter-bug."

Gensi watched as her sister disappeared from sight. Despite Aster's snobby grown-up airs, she missed her immediately. She thought she'd never had such a sad thing happen to her in her whole life. She decided it was all because of old Dessie, old smarty, farty Dessie. If Aster would only stay at home and play with her, she would excuse her for almost anything.

She really didn't care about playing with old Dessie anyhow. All old Dessie wanted to do was play jokes on her. The saddest thing of all was that Aster stood by and let her.

Her feelings still smarted from yesterday when she had followed Aster. Aster made her hide her eyes while Dessie dug a hole and put some real pretty flowery weeds on top of it.

Then Dessie said, "Gensi, if you want to find something real good, just dig in this hole."

She really knew better than to dig into that old hole, but when Aster said, "Do it, Gensi, do it," she did it, and got chick-en-shoo-ey all over her hands!

Gensi thought about visiting Ruby Wilkerson. She really, really liked Ruby because Ruby liked to laugh and have fun. She was always huggin' Jay Sky's neck. Sometimes when she hugged him a lot, his face got red. She could ask Ruby to play her favorite song on the Victrola; *I'm Walking The Floor Over You*. Maybe this time Ruby would tell her who was under that floor!

Getting to her feet, Gensi yawned and stretched. Ruby's house was too far away to go without asking Granny's permission. Granny would say she didn't need to go anyhow, then tell her she didn't have any business hanging around someone that lifted her skirt for a living, whatever that meant. So now what was she going to do?

She crossed through the tall grass separating the Holler from the pecan orchard and lay flat on her back under one of the big pecan trees. Hoping for inspiration, she tried to make up some stories. When that didn't work, she looked at the sky through the leaves until her eyes hurt. That wasn't any fun either since Aster wasn't there to see who could do it the lon'gest. Sitting up, she methodically examined and scratched each of her mosquito bites, then spit on them and rubbed the saliva in so they'd stop itching. Sooner or later, she thought in smug satisfaction, Aster was gonna want to play with her. Maybe she would play with Aster, and maybe she wouldn't. Old smarty, farty Aster, old smarty, farty, pootin', tootin' Aster!

From time to time Gensi glanced toward the far end of the orchard, where she feared to go because of the old cemetery. She really wished she knew the little girl who lived just on the other side. As if the cemetery wasn't scary enough, the reputation of the little girl's grandpa stopped her from even thinking about paying them a visit.

The thought of Joe Longtree, whom she had never seen, sent shivers down Gensi's spine. How many times had she heard Aster say, "You stop that now Gensi, or old Joe will come and git'che for sure. If old Joe Longtree is mean enough to shoot off his own toes, what do you think he would do to YOU?"

Joe Longtree was, indeed, a dark brooding, vicious bear of a man. The devil reincarnate, or so most of the Holler thought. Ever since, in a drunken fit of rage, he had shot off the toes of his right foot, his body had gone to fat, and his health along with it. Everyone speculated, without knowing for certain since no one had seen him in years, that Joe spent his days drinking, shooting off his gun, cursing, and yelling his head off at his wife, Catie. As for Catie, she had extra responsibility thrown on her since her daughter Vera, who was about as mean as Joe, got pregnant and dumped the baby into Catie's lap. Catie named the baby Lacy.

For Vera, that was the end of it. Catie reckoned little Lacy had no father, at least not one Vera could name, but she never had the nerve to ask. Nevertheless, Catie loved her granddaughter. She was furiously protective of her and always kept her by her side.

The Longtrees lived in a huge army tent, pitched in a secluded spot just below the old, seldom-if-ever used City Cemetery. Somehow, Catie had managed to put together a lean-to with cast-offs from the city dump. She attached this extension on the front of the tent, in order to keep as far away from Joe as she possibly could. Joe allowed her to move the kitchen into the lean-to only because it made the tent a cooler place for him.

Catie, a small woman with thin straggly hair, had to make calls to the Holler on a daily basis to fetch Joe his "medicine." Sometimes, Catie bargained for a bottle with a few eggs or a pint of wild berries. Mostly, she had to ask for credit. The twins knew that she did this to save face because she'd never have the money to pay for the moonshine. It didn't matter to them. They said many times that they'd trade with her anytime of the day for anything, including a sack of rocks, if it would help poor old Catie keep peace with Joe.

Up to this point, Gensi and Lacy had only stared at each other from behind their granny's skirt tails. Gensi was always curious about Lacy, but every time she asked Granny if she could play with her, Granny would say something like, "best to let sleepin' dogs die." Or something that didn't make any sense. Lacy didn't even have a dog.

Inch by inch, Gensi ventured closer and closer to the end of the orchard in hopes of seeing Lacy. Miffed at Aster, she skipped along the path for a ways, trying hard to think of something to make herself feel better. So deep was she into her sorrow that she didn't realize just how far down the path she had gone until all of a sudden she rounded a big row of bushes, and there was the dreaded graveyard smack-dab in front of her. She stopped skipping and breathing all at the same time.

The ancient headstones seemed to grow larger, and Gensi would swear they were movin' closer to her as they gleamed in the morning sun. Why any minute, she just knew, she would see a ghost rising up out of the graves, eager to gobble her up. She knew they were there; Aster had told her so.

Gensi tried as hard as she could to shake off the paralysis that gripped her. She wanted to run for her life but all of a sudden she saw something sure enough movin' on the other side of the cemetery.

"It's the ghost!" she screamed. "It's comin' to get me!" She just knew she was gonna pee all over herself. Then she realized it wasn't a ghost, but the little girl who lived on the other side of the cemetery.

"My name is Lacy," she heard the girl called timidly. "What's your name?"

"Gensi."

"Do you want to play?"

"I guess so."

Both girls stared at the cemetery. Neither wanted to cross the imaginary line. To do so would surely put them in peril of the dreaded haints.

"If you run real fast, they can't catch you," Lacy advised in a singsong voice.

Gensi's desire to play, plus curiosity about her new found acquaintance, prompted her to do the unthinkable. Taking a deep breath of courage, she clutched the front of her underwear trying not to pee on herself, then ran as fast as she could. By the time she reached Lacy, her little hinny had tried to get in front of her at least three times.

Lacy Longtree was a handsome, half-Indian child, tall and slender and the same age as Gensi.

It didn't take very long for the two little girls to become fast friends. Catie Longtree was busy scraping at the weeds surrounding the lean-to. She paused, leaned on her hoe handle, and listened. She was sure she heard voices coming from the direction of the cemetery. Feeling a bit uneasy, Catie dropped the hoe and went in search of Lacy. The sight before her delighted the old woman's heart. Sitting in the middle of the path playing jacks with her granddaughter Lacy was little Gensi Sinclair.

From that day on whenever pootin', tootin' Aster went off to play with old smarty, farty Dessie, Gensi sneaked off and braved the graveyard to play with her new friend, out of the sight of everyone but Catie Longtree.

All too soon, summer was over and it was time for Gensi to start to school. She knew that Aster went to school, but she had never planned to go herself. She figured she would just hang around in the Holler, play with Lacy, and go fishing with Jay Sky and Pebo. But Mama said she had to go. She thought again about her miss-placed bladder. If she cried long and loud enough, maybe she wouldn't have to go.

On the big day, the Holler kids, some clean and bright as new pennies, along with those not so clean and still reeking from either urinating on themselves or having slept with a sibling that did, assembled at the end of the path for the trek to the schoolhouse.

No matter how hard Gensi squalled and pulled back, Aster took her by the hand and, since she was larger, drug her all the way there. At school, Gensi saw her friend Lacy Longtree and suddenly everything was just fine.

That very afternoon, Robert made a house call in the vicinity of the school. No sooner had he parked his car than he heard a commotion. He turned just in time to see ten-year old Donnie Vendell charge Gensi with his bicycle, knocking her off the road into the ditch. To his surprise, Aster gave the wheel of the bicycle a vicious kick, knocking Donnie onto the ground. Then she jumped on top of him, grabbed him by the shirt collar and punched him in the nose. Before Robert could figure out who was winning, he saw Donnie riding toward him as fast as he could.

"Shithead! Shithead! You dirty old stinkin' shithead!" Aster yelled after him.

Donnie gave a final look over his shoulder just in case she was following him. Then he took a quick look around, hoping that none of his friends could see that he was crying.

Robert placed his medical bag on the hood of the car and waited until Donny Ray rode by. Stepping out, he grabbed the handlebars of the bicycle and brought him to a halt. Donny Ray gaped at Robert in surprise. A look of cunning crossed his face. He was sure he had found an ally in the doctor. "Did you see that? Did you see Aster Sinclair hit me, Dr. Vaughn?"

"Yes, I saw you get punched in the nose, little man, and you well deserved it. You should be ashamed of yourself for deliberately running into that little girl with your bicycle."

"What do you care?" he sneered between sobs. While wiping snot all over his face, he added, "They ain't nothin' but old Holler rats—my daddy said so."

"I care," Robert said, "and when I finish speaking to your father and the school, so will you. Now, go home."

Tears of shame and humiliation burned Gensi's eyes as Aster pulled her out of the ditch. All of the kids were laughing at her and, on top of that, scary old Dr. Vaughn was watching her. She kept her head down and tried desperately not to cry.

As protectively as a watchdog, Aster stood beside her little sister. Her chestnut hair, as wild as her mother's, whipped about her face. Standing her ground with eyes glaring and fists tightly clenched at her side; she dared any of the on-lookers to take her on.

As Robert walked toward the girls, admiration welled inside of him for the spunk he had seen displayed by this little girl. Grass stains marred the front of Aster's white blouse, which was missing several buttons, and hanging off one shoulder.

Blood was running down Gensi's right leg, and a red welt burned on her cheek. She gave a swipe at her cheek, leaving a dirty streak.

After sending the other children on their way, Robert squatted in front of Gensi. Taking his handkerchief, he cleaned her nose. "Here," he said soothingly, "let me take a look at that scratch." He cleaned it and removed a bottle of iodine from his medical bag. "This might burn a little," he cautioned.

Gensi squenched her face and gave out a yelp when he dabbed the scrape with the iodine. Then he blew on it until she opened her eyes –as green as grass and so very much like his mother's that it gave him a jolt.

Gensi's lower lip quivered. Despite her best efforts not to cry, a big tear oozed out and slid down her cheek. Gently, he wiped it away.

Still glaring after Donny Ray, Aster reassured him. "It's okay, Dr. Vaughn. I punched him in the nose."

Robert nodded as he attended to a scrape on this heroic little girl's elbow. "I know you did Aster. I bet he'll think twice before he tangles with you again."

"He called us Holler rats. I called him a shithead," she told him.

A smile tugged at the corners of his mouth. He stood up, towering over the little girl with a freckled nose, whose tiny fists were still clenched, ready to do battle. For the first time it hit him what a burden this small child carried. He glanced at Gensi. The realization troubled him. The shame and guilt he felt, he couldn't suppress, no matter how hard he tried. Not only was Aster a Holler rat, she had to defend *his child* from the same stigma. For the first time in his life, he hung his head in shame.

"Aster," he was finally able to say, "as an adult, I suppose it's my duty to tell you that your language is not appropriate for a young lady." He patted her on the head and let his eyes follow the escape route Donny Ray had taken. "However, after giving it considerable thought," he added, "I think you're right."

Encouraged, Aster said, "Cross your heart and hope to die?"

"Cross my heart and hope to die, Aster. Now how about a ride home?"

Both little girls readily agreed.

The pain Robert was feeling was the beginning of a tiny crack in the wall he had built around his heart. A crack that might possibly grow, at least for the child he had conveniently ignored, if he would let it.

Chapter 25
To Conspire

An all night rain across southeast Missouri brought the first break from the stifling heat of late summer. The air—clean, cools, and refreshing, whipped the folds of Willa Sinclair's skirt and wound the wild mass of chestnut hair around her face and neck. With one hand on her thigh, she held the rust-colored skirt of rayon crepe against her slender body and freed her hair with the other. Tossing her head ever so slightly, she allowed the mane to be lifted by the exhilarating breeze.

"Good morning, Willa," James Shaw called to her as they passed on the sidewalk, his voice deep and pleasant. The smile he always had for her spread across his near handsome face. He splayed his fingers and ran them through the cap of unruly auburn hair that always needed combing. Then he turned to go.

Willa watched him stroll to his office. He had an easy loose-limbed gait, a perfect match to his imperturbable manner. It was the sad expression in his soft amber eyes, which caused her to wonder. She watched him unlock the door to the old brick building.

Glancing over his shoulder, Shaw removed something from under his jacket before disappearing inside his office.

Willa forced her mind from James Shaw to the events of the morning. "This is going to be one of those days, I can feel it in my bones," she grumbled as she crossed the street to the post office. Already she had made two deliveries of medicine to people as able to retrieve it as she was to deliver it.

Without formalities, a voice from the past interrupted Robert as he sat at his desk studying medical records. "My, my, you haven't changed a bit. I do declare to you here and now that I think you're the handsomest man I've ever met."

A frown crossed Robert's face for being disturbed during his private time. It was quickly replaced by a look of surprise.

Tall, leggy Sara Jane Lockwood Whittingham, who had apparently not given up on being a Joan Bennett look-a-like, stood in the door as beautifull, groomed as ever.

"Really now, Sara Jane, I might have believed that line when you were a school girl, and I a much younger man." He rounded his desk and greeted her warmly. Taking her by both hands, he kissed her on the cheek. "I must say you are looking good. Home for a visit?" He directed her to a chair.

Sara Jane was wearing a clever toque hat which, she was quick to point out to anyone dare they infer otherwise, was an original from Paris, France. She seated herself and waited until Robert propped himself on the desk directly in front on her.

"More like home for a divorce," she said. Extending her right ankle in front of him, she made an elaborate pretense of checking the seams on her fashionable silk stockings. While doing so, she managed to brush Robert's outer thigh with her knee.

None too discretely, putting the desk between them, Robert replied, "I'm sorry to hear that."

"Oh, don't be, I'm not," Sara Jane replied, rather too forcefully.

"Do you have any children?" he asked, feeling a need to change the direction of the conversation.

"No children, and it's for the best. Les Whittingham was a good enough man, I suppose. I just wasn't in love with him." Shrugging her shoulders, Sara Jane removed her gloves, then, with long lacquered fingernails, pushed back the diamond bracelet, which had been cut specifically for her.

Finishing her rounds, Willa hurried from the post office into the Merchant and Planter Bank and then back across the street to find Robert's car still in its parking space. He should be on his way by now to see Mattie Vandiver, she thought. She made a face at the clock on the wall, dropped the mail on the front desk, and hurried into his office.

"I took Rose Marie Long her...Oh, I'm sorry, I thought you were free." Without checking out the visitor, she backed out of the room.

"Wait," Robert called, rose and quickly made his way around the desk. "You remember Sara Jane, don't you?" he asked Willa, a slight hint of mockery in his voice.

"Well, of course, I remember her," Willa said sweetly. "So nice of you to stop by. How in the world are you, Sara Jane?"

Before Sara Jane answered, she measured Willa. Doing better than you, her eyes seemed to say.

Willa fingered the button on the tailored broadcloth blouse from the National Bella Hess catalog and took Sara Jane's measure. Nothing ever changes, she thought.

Turning to Robert she said, "I'm afraid you're going to have to cut this visit with your *old* friend short. You were expected to be at the Vandiver's house ten minutes ago."

Sara Jane's eyes glittered in the old way. "Well..." she quipped, as she tapped the end of a cigarette on a gold monogrammed case.

Before she could finish the sentence or light up, Robert stretched his hand out to her, "I'm really sorry, Sara Jane, but duty calls." Escorting her to the front door, he insisted, "We'll get together and visit another time."

Willa opened the door and smiled sweetly as Sara Jane passed through it. After she closed the door, she privately offered a curt, "Good riddance." Deciding it was no time to discuss Sara Jane, she stifled the urge.

"The day hasn't even started, and we're falling behind already," she told Robert as she handed him his bag and ushered him out the side door.

Due to an outbreak of a stomach virus, the day only got worse. When the last patient finally passed through the doors after many grueling hours of complaints and misery, Willa gave a sigh of relief, then frowned as the telephone rang in her ears.

"Who may I say is calling?" she asked the caller, even though she had recognized Sara Jane's voice.

"Why should I tell you? It's after hours."

"You'll tell me if you wish to speak to the doctor," Willa snapped.

Robert, guessing whom the caller might be, reached to take the phone from her, only to discover Willa turned her back on him and tried to butt him out of the way. He was not to be ignored, it was his practice, after all, and insisted on having the phone.

"Guess who this is?" Sara Jane purred.

"I know who it is," he answered, making his voice as deep, husky, and sexy as possible.

"Are you pleased to hear from me so soon?"

"Am I pleased?" Watching Willa's facial reaction, he added, "If I were to place the receiver over my heart, you could hear it pounding."

Willa rolled her eyes. "Good grief," she muttered.

"I'm sorry I had to cut our visit short, this morning," he told her. "I've got a great idea how to make it up to you. Why don't you bring those long legs of yours to my office, let's say around six o'clock? You can curl them in one of my easy chairs and have a drink with me for old time's sake."

"Well of all things," she giggled. "What *would* people think?"

"To hell with people."

"Be careful what you say," she cautioned. "If I remember correctly, the telephones around here have ears."

At that moment, they both heard a click, confirming that Betty Russell, the telephone operator, had indeed been listening. And so the conversation went until Willa had heard enough and walked out of the room.

Hanging up the phone, Robert stuck his hands into his pockets and casually strolled into the examining room. "Mrs. Sinclair," he stated, "would you be so kind as to get me a bottle of gin and a couple of glasses before you leave? As you know, Sara Jane is…"

Cutting him short, Willa said, "You might as well save your breath, Romeo, because *I ain't* getting them for you!" Grabbing her purse, she headed for the door.

"It seems you've forgotten something, Mrs. Sinclair," he stated in a voice cold as ice. "You work for me, and I give the orders."

She leaned against the front door. "Perhaps it's you that's forgotten something. I'm not your maid anymore."

Robert's eyes narrowed. "Are you refusing a direct order?"

"Well. I guess I am," she said emphatically.

"Then you're fired."

"Fine!" she shouted and opened the door.

In two long strides, Robert crossed the room, closed the door, and locked it. He pulled down the shades before grabbing her by the arms and drawing Willa in front of him. "Now let's get one thing straight, Mrs. Sinclair. You're not going anywhere until we've settled this."

"Firing me sounded pretty settling to me," she sneered.

He pulled her against him, breathing her scent deep into his lungs. It had been so long since he had touched her that his fingers were visibly trembling. His voice softened. "Fire you, not on your life," he whispered against her ear. Before she could pull away, he caught her head in his hands, kissing her until she melted against him.

"Have you forgotten," she managed to ask, "about Lady Sara Jane?"

"It appears," he murmured, "that I need to get in touch with her." He let his moist tongue trail down Willa's neck. "And huh, you will, I am sure vouch for me if necessary ..." he paused, worked the buttons on her blouse, and slid his hand inside " ...that I have this emergency on my hands." He found her breast warm and aroused.

Willa's breath quickened. "Yes, an emergency," she breathed and closed her eyes. Here she was doing it again, blindly descending headlong into the forbidden.

Robert lowered his head to her breast. How he had longed for this...

The tugging she felt rendered her incapable of caring about anything other than him.

"Yes, oh-h, yes," she whispered, as his hand moved up her thigh, "we *definitely* have an emergency."

Chapter 26
Life

On a Sunday afternoon, several men, including Ben Melton and the Higgers' boys, sat under the large cottonwood tree, smokin', chewin', spittin', and watchin' as barges, loaded with everything from cattle to folks with all their belongings, floated down the river.

The older women, as was the custom, sat separately on the front porch of one of the Higgers boys' shacks.

Willa Sinclair and Ruby Wilkerson, out of ear shot but still under scrutiny of the older women, settled themselves on the small boat dock, which extended out into the river.

Slipping her shoes off, Ruby stuck the tip of her toes into the still icy water. Then she let out a squeal, which promptly brought looks of disapproval from Maw NanEmmer, and Effie Melton.

Not the least bit contrite, she made a big splash before jerking her feet out of the water. Leaning back on her hands, Ruby gave her head a toss so that her honey blond hair spilled around her shoulders. She gazed at Willa, giving her a knowing look, she said, "Go ahead, spill you guts girl. That's why we're here, ain't it?"

Willa drew her knees up under her chin and wrapped her arms around them. "I guess so," she mumbled. "The problem is, I don't seem to know where to begin."

Ruby grinned. "First," she said, "try admitting to me, that you're *doin'it* again with the good doctor." When Willa didn't answer, Ruby added, "Well, aren't you?"

Willa took a deep breath. Nodding her head, she spread her hands. "Can you believe it?" she whispered, "after six long years."

Ruby drew one leg up under her and for several long seconds, seemed to be contemplating the depths of the water. At last, she faced Willa and took a deep breath. "So," she exhaled slowly. "Are you telling me that you're sorry?"

Willa frowned, and screwed her features into a grimace. "Well not exactly." She cautiously placed her hands on the splintery boards covering the dock and carefully scooted around until she was facing Ruby. "I'm going to try to tell you something, Ruby, that I don't think I could bring myself to ever admit to anyone else." Willa took a deep breath. "When he touches me," her speech faltered—how could she explain to her friend that when she was with Robert, how one kiss could undermine her judgment to the point that she didn't care about the consequences. She began again. "He…Robert makes me feel so…so alive, and at the same time as though I'm—I'm—" she threw up her hands in desperation as she searched her mind for a suitable word, "drowning," she blurted out. Then, after giving Ruby a quizzical glance, she added, "Does that make any sense to you?"

Ruby's brow rose, and in an ever-so-proper voice, she stated, "Have you forgotten to *whom* you are speaking?" After a righteous burst of laugher and another glare from the older women, Willa went on. "But wouldn't you think that after six years, it would be different with us? But the truth is, nothing has changed. If anything, it's worse than ever. We can't seem to get enough of each other." She grimaced. "I swear to you Ruby, before I can get my clothes back on, he's acting as though it never happened." Willa closed her eyes and whispered. "At one point in my life, just knowing he wanted me was enough. But now, I want more, Ruby. I want to know if he cares about more than just my body, and I want him to tell me so. Is that asking too much?"

Ruby chunked a clod of dirt into the river. "Have you ever asked him how he feels about you?"

"Gosh, no!"

"Then maybe you should."

Willa grunted, "I wish it was that simple. To be perfectly honest, I don't have the guts."

"Me neither," Ruby added in a dry voice. A sad look crossed her normally merry face. "As strange as it may seem, we're sort'a in the same boat, kid'o." Pulling an imaginary flower from out of the air, she pretended to pluck the pedals. "Jay Sky loves me, he loves me not," she said flatly.

"Well, Miss Smartie, since you just as well said that Jay Sky has never told you how he feels, how do you know so much?"

"It's simple. Unlike the good doctor, I know, and you know, that if Jay Sky loved me, he would tell me so." Ruby studied Willa's face for several seconds. "The way I see it, Willa, is just be happy with what'che got. I reckon you could call that my motto since I repeat it to myself several times a day. I can't tell you what's right for you. For me, living in the present seems to work best. One could argue that from mine and Jay Sky's activities," she said with a sardonic laugh, "I work overtime trying to store up as much happiness as I possibly can." After a few seconds of silence she add. "What it boils down to, friend-of-mine, is I take what Jay Sky has to give me and with a humongous appetite." She glanced at her friend. "And I suspect that, that is precisely what you've been doing, isn't it?"

"I suppose so," Willa said, in a hushed tone. "But it's just not enough anymore."

A little further down the river, Justin sat on the steps of the Sky House and read the letter for a second time. He balled the paper in his hands and stared at it. It doesn't matter how many times I read it, he thought, it's not going to change. He smoothed it out and returned it to the envelope. There was no way around it; he was being drafted into the Army.

When Pebo finished bathing, he settled himself alongside Justin. "Hou, Brave Rider," he said.

Justin took in a ragged breath and looked at him with the strangest expression that Pebo had ever seen. They sat in silence for several moments, until Pebo, feeling uncomfortable, began to squirm. Maybe Jay Sky was mad at him. He was just about to say he was sorry, even though he didn't know what he had done, when Jay Sky placed his hand on his arm.

"I want to tell you something," Justin said, "and you must listen as carefully as you possibly can."

Relieved that Jay Sky wasn't mad at him, Pebo bobbed his head up and down and drew his brow together to show how hard he was trying.

"I've been telling you for sometime that I might have to go away."

Pebo's heart fell. He vaguely remembered hearing a little about some folks having a fight somewheres away off, and that Jay Sky might have to help stop it. Jay Sky had also told him that he wouldn't have to go until he got an in-duck....Pebo struggled to think of the word. It didn't make any sense to him. His eyes shifted to the letter Justin held in his hands. "You ain't suppose to fight," he said.

"You're right, buddy." Justin cleared his throat. "You and I had a talk about the Philippines, just last week, remember?"

He lowered his head in thought. The field-of-beans, the field-of-beans. Sure, sure, he knew all about the field-of-beans. He'd even talked it over with Aster and Gensi, but none of 'em could understand why Jay Sky was gonna have to go and straighten out problems in some old field-of-beans!

"Well," Justin added, "I'll probably be sent there and that's a far piece from here, which means I'll be gone for a long while."

Pebo's head dropped to his chest. His heart was breaking. Damn old field-of-beans. He didn't think he could ever eat beans again. But then, he reasoned, if he didn't eat any more beans, he might get hungry since that was about all there was to eat most days in the Holler.

Justin's voice broke through Pebo's preoccupation, "Are you listening to me, buddy?"

"I'm listin'," Pebo said glumly.

"This is between you and me. Do you think you can remember not to tell anyone until I tell them first?"

Pebo raised his tear-filled eyes and gazed at Justin Rider with the misery of a heart-broken, confused child written on his face. His world stopped at the city limits of Hornersville. He might not understand as much as Jay Sky wanted him to understand, but he knew enough to know that his world was changing. Jay Sky was leaving. He didn't know if he could live without him. "Ok, Jay Sky, best buddy," he whispered, "oo-kay."

Justin pulled himself to his feet. "I have several things to do this morning, things that I need to do alone. I'll see you later," he whispered and walked away.

Pebo's tears were flowing freely now, and his hands were gesticulating. He had to do something. The pain was more than he could tolerate. He beat his mighty fist into the soft earth at his side and repeated some of Aster's favorite words. "Hot-damn, shit, som-a-bitch!" he said again and again. By this time his huge frame had doubled over, and he was sobbing like the child he would always be.

On the day of Justin's departure, Willa and the girls watched through the kitchen window until they saw him crossing the Holler.

Slowly, Gensi backed away from the window and quietly slipped out of the house to hide herself between the knees of the old cypress tree.

"Gensi," he called, his voice deep and gentle.

Gensi didn't answer; she rolled over and buried her face deep into her ragged old quilt.

Jay Sky stooped as low as his tall frame would allow, lowered his head, and arched a black brow. "I can't believe you're not going to say good-by to me."

"I don't want you to go," she answered, her voice muffled.

"And I don't want to go, you know that." As he squatted down, his heels raised up and he balanced himself on the tips of his toes. "I've already explained to you that I don't have any choice in the matter. Remember your first day of school? You didn't want to go, but despite how you felt, you had to go. Well, this is one of those times for me. Regardless of how I feel about going, I have to go. If I don't go, Gensi, they might just come and get me and put me in jail, and I'd be a dishonorable man. Worst of all, Gensi, I'd be a dishonorable Indian brave. You wouldn't want that now, would you?" He could see her looking at him out of the corner of her eye.

"Why do things have to change?" she blurted out in anger.

"Because they must, baby. Most of the time, things change in small ways, and we don't notice until something really big happens."

He hung his head and looked as dejected as he possibly could. "It's time for me to go," he whispered. "It's just plain gonna break my heart having to leave like this without my favorite girl giving me a hug."

In a blink of an eye, Gensi was in his arms. "I love you," she cried, hugging him fiercely. "I love you so much, Jay Sky."

"I love you too, Gensi. Now promise me you'll be a good girl while I'm gone," he said huskily.

"I promise," she answered, giving him a snotty kiss.

As Jay Sky left the Holler, he turned around for one last goodbye. First he waved to Willa standing on the porch, then to Gensi under the old cypress tree. He quickly scanned the yard for Aster and found that she had crawled under the house. Feeling that he may have slighted her, he called back. "Aster, will you make me a promise?"

He could vaguely see the movement of a knot of hair under the floorboards.

"Promise that you won't use dirty words while I'm gone."

"I promise, Jay Sky, I truly promise," Aster cried, and this time, she intended to try with all of her heart to stick to it.

Chapter 27
We Make Known

For many years, the one that got away had served as a source of irritation to Sara Jane's ego. And her persistent desire for Robert Vaughn, along with flirtatious exploits with numerous other men, contributed to the demise of her marriage.

Her face clothed in a mask of determination, she slipped into a black dress of Canton crepe, which she especially chose for this occasion because of the way the sixteen-gore shirt deliciously showed off, in vibrant detail, the curve of her slim hips.

"He's right about one thing," she said. "I'm definitely not a schoolgirl any longer."

Sara Jane had hoped that, on her return to Hornersville, she would find Willa Sinclair to be a thing of the past. Observing herself in the dressing mirror in the bedroom of her childhood, she slipped on the matching two-inch Cuban pumps. That gal's a problem, she admitted to herself. But of course, Willa wasn't the first obstacle she had encountered over the years, and more often than not, she'd gotten what she wanted.

"Many have fallen by the wayside. I pride myself in taking no prisoners," she giggled. She drew her stomach in and drummed her fingers on her flat belly. "As they say in advertising, my girl, it's all in the presentation."

Sitting on the sofa, nursing yet another a stiff drink of the early Sunday evening, Robert Vaughn mused on his life. He quaffed down the rest of the drink and stared at the bottom of the empty glass. These days, it seemed his feelings of guilt were transcending the antidote. He reached for a refill.

"What a miserable life you've created for yourself," he said aloud. "You're an asshole to boot, a certified asshole, yes sir-ree." Bone weary from the mess he'd made, he laid his head back and drifted off.

Awakened by the clanging of the doorbell, he groaned, pulled himself to his feet, and stumbled to the door.

When he opened it, Sara Jane, holding a fresh apple pie in her hands, swept past him toward the kitchen, not even waiting to be invited inside. Calling back over her shoulder as he went, she announced, "Mama sent this."

Bowing to the empty doorway, Robert besottedly gave a wave of his arm. "Come right on in, Sara Jane," he said, drained the glass, and pitched it onto the sofa. "Using the old pie trick again, aren't you?" he muttered to himself. "Not very original, my dear." Using the walls to steady himself, he followed her to the kitchen. Leaning against the door for support, he attempted to show his appreciation, "Thank your mother for the..." Before he could finish his statement, Sara Jane had wrapped herself around him and was grinding her body against his.

Willa Sinclair slipped out of the Holler as she often did when the girls stayed overnight with Ben and Effie. Avoiding the main streets of town, she stole noiselessly through the gate, onto the back porch of Robert's house and opened the door. Her face paled at the sight of Robert, in the shadow of the dimly lit kitchen, holding Sara Jane in his arms.

Sara Jane's lipstick-smeared mouth promptly twisted into a malicious smile.

Robert, looking dumfounded, gazed at Willa. "What are you doing here?" he demanded.

"It seems I should have made an appointment," she said and fled.

Robert followed her to the back porch, leaned his head against the door screen, and closed his eyes.

Joining him, Sara Jane placed her hands on his shoulders. Feeling a sense of triumph, she let them trail down his back and around his waist. Moving closer, she whispered. "Where were we before we were so rudely interrupted?"

The muscle in his right cheek began to twitch, a sure sign of agitation. Removing her hands from his body, he turned to face her. "I think it's time for you go," he said.

"Go?"

"I'm sorry, Sara Jane, but this has been a mistake."

"A mistake?" she shrieked.

Robert nodded grimly.

Sara Jane's eyebrows raised in awareness. "Oh, I see," she said with a sneer. "It's because of Willa Sinclair."

Robert studied her for several long seconds, wondering how he could have ever, even for a few seconds, felt passion for her. "It's not because of Mrs. Sinclair. I'm refusing you because you don't interest me," he stated bluntly. "I never wanted you before you were married, and I don't want you now. I'm sorry to be so blunt, Sara Jane, but you just don't seem to get it." He took her by the arm and led her to the door.

Sara Jane swung around. "You're not half as sorry as you're going to be," she hissed, then slammed the door in his face.

"Sara Jane, the kissing bug, the assassin bug," he moaned, "bloodsucking and poisonous, biting its victims on the lips."

True to her word, Sara Jane spent the next few days spreading rumors.

To commiserate for Sara Jane, Jackie Vendell quickly planned an unscheduled meeting for the garden club.

Sara Jane and her mother were the first to arrive. After being strategically seated on the horsehair sofa, Sara Jane, looking prim and proper in a simple two-piece frock described as Peter Pan in Polka-land, which under any other circumstance she wouldn't be caught dead in, held a hankie in her hand.

Not one soul who received an invitation failed to show, and for the first time in history, everyone was on time. After tea and cucumber sandwiches, the group grew quiet with anticipation.

Sara Jane took a deep breath and placed her hand dramatically onto her breast. "This is going to be very hard for me, so I hope that you'll bear with me," she said, dabbing at her downcast eyes. "This is not hearsay, you understand, because I would never be caught spreading a falsehood. I know for a fact," she said taking a deep breath, "that our doctor and Willa Sinclair are lovers." In sanctimonious tones, she related how she, on an errand for her mother, happened to be an eyewitness to the fact.

"Well, it certainly wasn't your fault, dear," Jackie Vendell said.

Dorothy Lockwood touching the throat of her new navy blue chiffon dress in righteous indignation leaned forward and patted her daughter's hand. "I can't believe that I actually encouraged you to deliver that pie."

Sara Jane rolled her eyes, nodded her dark head crowned in a hat called Pixie Peak, and affected an involuntary shudder.

Dorothy placed her arms around her daughter who was doing her best to look as if sin had never touched her. "Why Sara Jane has been so mortified by the turn of events that she hasn't had a decent night's rest since it happened."

Jackie Vendell bedecked in two-pieced linen, gracefully gored, nodded her head and reiterated, "It certainly wasn't your fault, dear."

Erna Cade, so skinny she could hardly cast a shadow, had waited as she always did until everyone had had her say. Knowing that the community considered her as beyond reproach, and one who only spoke words of wisdom, she couldn't help but be concerned with the possibility of the town losing their doctor if this scandal was viewed as his doings.

"Let's not be so hasty to blame the doctor," she said receiving more tea. "I'm sure if we knew the straight of it, the brazen hussy laid a trap for him."

The very austere Mary Ellen Watkins, as usual so bound up in a rubber reducer girdle that it threatened to cut off her breath should she relax or devour an eleventh cucumber sandwich, followed her friend's lead and declared, "And let us not forget, ladies, not for one moment, that he's a man."

"Well! Then we really can't blame the doctor, can we?" Erna interjected. "Men are expected to transgress, especially when it's being rubbed in their face."

"Come to think of it…."

With viperous tongues, each took a turn relating how they had seen things about Willa that, of course, they hadn't thought much about at the time but now, since it had been brought to their attention . . .. On and on the gossip went.

For several days after the tea, the good ladies of Hornersville tied up the telephone lines, completely wearing to a frazzle poor Betty Russell, the telephone operator, as she tried not to miss a single word of gossip.

The Holler ladies, although more tolerant of Willa, were not above gossiping about her. Instead of calling a tea to dissect the situation as the town women did, they simply met over the clothesline. On several occasions, when they were quite positive that Effie Melton wasn't around, they came together on the porch of someone's shack to discuss the latest gossip about Willa and Dr. Vaughn.

It was on such an occasion, that Vernie Higgers offered a possible explanation for Willa's actions. "I heard about this operation," she said in deepest confidence. "I don't know its name, but it's when the doctors ...clean you out."

Several of the ladies, just to show how knowledgeable they were about such things, nodded their heads.

"Well," Vernie said, "they tell me when a woman has one of 'em, it makes her crazy about...*you know*..." she glanced around to make sure none of the men or children were listening, "...about *it,*" she whispered.

"What's that got to do with Willa?" her twin, Mernie, demanded.

Exasperated at her sister for being so thick headed, Vernie scolded. "Well Mernie, don't you see? Him be'n a doctor and all, it may be that he cleaned her out without her even knowin' it."

Monday morning, Willa was determined to finish her usual routine of errands around town for the doctor, despite the fact that Doris Ross at the bank had already looked at her, as her mama would say, "like she was about to fit and fall back in it." Then on the way out, the normally friendly Megan Holmes had actually looked the other way to keep from speaking.

Willa crossed the street right in front of attorney James Shaw's office and unfortunately came face to face with Tammy Dees and Dinah Black. By the time Tammy and Dinah had had their say, Willa knew in no uncertain terms that her secret was out. She had been told just how ashamed of herself she should feel.

When it seemed that matters could not get any worse, Willa opened the door to the post office to find Sara Jane holding court. All eyes shifted in Willa's direction. For a second, Willa considered not going in, but thought, hell, no; I won't give them the satisfaction of seeing me run. She took a deep breath, lifted her head, and walked to the wall of mailboxes to work the combination on box 191.

"Well if it isn't the town's strumpet!" Sara Jane hissed.

Willa stiffened but never stopped what she was doing. After gathering up the mail, she took a deep breath and turned to leave.

"Wahhhh-whoooo, wahhhh-whoooo," floated across the room, followed by sniggering.

Willa froze.

"Square your shoulders, young lady," he said close to her ear. "Hold up your head and let me see you smile as if I just said something quite funny." He waited until Willa lifted her head and made an effort at smiling. Taking her by the arm, he casually escorted her toward the post office door. "Not that I'm noted for my sense of humor," he went on, "but then again—what do they know? I might just be funny as hell."

The laugh he provoked in her was quite genuine this time.

"Well, did you ever?" Sara Jane stated. "I guess now she's after James Shaw!"

When they reached his office, he motioned Willa to a chair.

"I suppose you know that you may have just ruined your reputation," she said, not meeting his eyes.

"Thank you for your concern," he answered as he settled his loose frame into the chair behind his desk. "But I don't have a reputation to worry about since I never found time to cultivate that part of my life."

"Well, I thank you for what you did, anyway." After a short pause, she added, "You know it's true, don't you?" When he didn't answer, she continued. "I don't mean the way Sara Jane is telling it, but...basically, it's true. My mama always said to always tell the truth," Willa went on after James did not respond, "because the truth will never hurt you." Picking at an imaginary bit of lint on the front of her dress, she asked. "Do you know my mama?"

"Yes, I do. As a matter of fact, I've bought soap from her on several occasions. I've always enjoyed our conversations."

"Then I don't have to tell you that my mama considers herself an authority on most things, and she's not often wrong. But if I dared, I could tell her first hand that there are times when the truth does hurt." Her voice broke and in a few seconds, tears were dripping from her chin.

James handed her his handkerchief.

Willa accepted the offer and before she knew what was happening, she found herself gazing into the most sympathetic eyes she had seen since Jay Sky had left for the Army, eyes filled not only with kindness but also strength and integrity. Unexpectedly, she was pouring her heart out to him.

"Have you ever been hungry, Mr. Shaw?" she asked insistently.

"Call me James, and yes," he said, "I guess I have, to a degree."

"You've always been able to appease your hunger, haven't you?"

"Pretty much so," he said.

"Before I married Billy Rider, I had never been inside of a restaurant. One Saturday night, he took me 'out to eat' as he called it. Billy was quite the magnanimous one that night. He handed me the menu. '*Order anything you like,*' he said." Willa smiled at James. "You'd never guess in a million years what I ordered. I ordered a bowl of chili. You know why?"

Of course he didn't know why. James also knew the question was rhetorical, so he didn't bother answering her. He didn't think she would have heard him if he did.

"Because the only thing on the menu that I knew anything about was chili. Boy, was I in for a shock. You see I really didn't know much about chili either. You know why?"

This time, James shook his head.

"Because all the chili I'd ever eaten had been watered down so that there'd be enough to go around, and it had very little flavor."

Willa took a deep breath, "I've been hungry all of my life," she stated, "a hunger that goes much deeper than for food. I guess what I am trying to say is that I hungered for Robert a long time before I knew he existed."

Pulling herself to her feet, Willa crossed the room. Reaching the door, she leaned her forehead against the cool windowpane. "As watered down as my relationship has been with Robert, it's more than I ever dreamed of having, but that's no excuse for my behavior."

Turning slightly, Willa knitted her brow into an expression of serious consideration. "Regardless of all that's happened, I honestly don't know if I'm strong enough to put an end to it. Can you understand that?" She searched his face. "For some reason, I want you to think well of me."

"I can understand, and I do think well of you, Willa," he said in a clearly uncomfortable voice. He cleared his throat, "You didn't ask for my opinion," he went on, "but if you don't mind, I'd like to go on record as saying that I feel you've been selling yourself short for all these years, mighty short."

"Thank you," she whispered as she walked out the door.

Therewith, James Shaw slumped deep into the chair. After a long while, he reached into the inside pocket of his vest, retrieved an item, studied it, then pressed it to his chest and closed his eyes. The memories came easily.

An all night rain had brought the first relief to southeast Missouri from the stifling heat of late summer...Parking his car, ready to disengage his long legs from under the steering column, he looks up and sees her...standing on the steps dreamily savoring the clean, cool, refreshing air. The wild tosses her mass of tangled chestnut hair, winding it around her face and neck. With his heart in his throat, he watches as she frees the glorious tresses. Then with a toss of her head, she releases them to the wind. His gasp is audible, as the expression on her face seems to project pure sensual pleasure. With heart pounding, he watches as the wind caresses her as deftly as any lover's hands...Without taking his eyes from her, he reaches for the camera on the car seat beside him.

Swallowing hard, James pulled himself upright in the chair and wrestled with his conscience. He had never let himself go beyond this point, and he didn't want to do it now. He shoved the article he held in his hand under a stack of papers. Grabbing up a brief, he tried to go over it. Seconds later, he realized he was halfway down the page, and he didn't know a damn thing about what he was reading. Tossing the document aside, he reached under the stack of papers, pulled out the picture, and leaned back in the chair. Guilt filled his chest. "God forgive me," he said. Thereupon, he placed the secret snapshot of Willa Sinclair over his heart and closed his eyes. At that time, the unflappable James Shaw surrendered to the emotion he had denied himself for so long. He allowed himself to imagine...*as he watches the wind caress and stroke her body...that he is the wind.*

Chapter 28
Done Conditionally

That evening in the Holler, Willa and her girls were having supper when they heard a squealing outside, akin to a wildcat tryin' to catch a rabbit. Flinging open the screen door, Willa rushed out to find Tucker Duzen, a recluse from down on the ditches, yelping and jumping up and down in the backyard. It didn't take a genius to figure out that something had gone terribly wrong. Tucker's face was about as red as his frizzled hair.

Willa placed her hand on his arm in an effort to calm him down and declared, "For heaven sakes, Duzen, what's wrong?"

"It's Lee! Miz Willa! My wife, Lee! She's a takin' on fiercely cause she can't have her young'n!" he cried as he twisted his hat around and around in his hands. "My maw, she's been tryin' to bring it, but it jest won't come! Lee's had young'ns a'fore, lot's of 'em, and maw's brung 'em all. But she scart about this'n, so she sent me to fetch you."

"Oh my!" Willa's mind raced. "Duzen," she said. "I know you don't like going into town, but you've got to go find Dr. Vaughn." Tucker Duzen backed off defensively. Realizing that Duzen didn't know where to find Robert, Willa said, "Hold on a minute." She turned to Aster. "Go get one of the Higger boys to go with him."

Aster took off running.

After Willa instructed him on what to do, Ricky Joe Higgers made several steps up the path and then realized that Duzen was not exactly following him. He gave Willa a pleading look.

"Go! Duzen," she commanded, giving him a shove. She would have loved to follow it up with a swift kick.

"What if the doctor won't come?" Tucker Duzen whined.

"He'll come. Ricky Joe, you tell him that Willa Sinclair sent for him, and that I said it is an emergency. Hurry! Hurry!" she hissed.

Ricky Joe took off in a run. Duzen reluctantly brought up the rear.

Willa grabbed as many clean towels and sheets as she could stuff into a flour sack. She turned to the two wide-eyed little girls, "Go stay with the Higgers until Mama and Papa get back," she said. "Tell them that I'm taking the boat and for them to see that the doctor gets down the river to Tucker Duzen's place as fast as possible."

Willa could hear the piercing screams of Lee Duzen long before she reached the dock in front of their pathetic three-room shack, with its ill-patched roof, broken windows, and sagging door.

"Please, please, be home, Robert!" she repeated over and over as she drew up to the bank and threw the rope to the oldest of the three boys standing there.

Hedy Duzen, Tucker's mama, stood in the yard wringing her hands. She was old and stooped and with hair as frizzled as Tucker's. With sharp eyes peering over her long nose, she watched as Willa made her way up the bank. "Who you be?'

"You know very well who I am, Hedy," Willa said sharply. "Now take me to Lee."

Hedy nodded her head. "I done did all I c'n do fer her. I seed that all the locks in the house be open, and I put an axe under her bed to cut the pain."

Willa gave Hedy a strange look.

"But she ain't doin' good," Hedy went on. "I seed two black birds a sittin' together the other day, and I know'd it was a bad sign. I told Lee so."

Of course you did, Willa thought. Trying to ignore the rest of Hedy's prophesying, Willa surveyed the conditions in which they lived. Another piercing scream from Lee forced Willa to stop being judgmental. Clutching her supplies, she rushed through the front room, past two smaller children huddled together on the cot in the corner behind the stove. About that time, one of the old coon dogs crawled through the crack in the floor, jumped up, and joined another asleep in the middle of one of the three unmade beds.

Hedy ushered Willa into a small, fetid room in the very back of the house that, like the rest of the place, reeked of filth.

Willa wanted to take a deep calming breath before she undertook the task at hand but wrinkled her nose and thought better of it. Glancing at Lee, she quickly decided that since she didn't know what she was doing, she would have to trick Lee into believing she did.

"Ok, Lee, let's have a look," she said in a professional tone she had often heard Robert use.

"Oh-h, Miz Willa, I ain't goin' to be able to have this'n. Maw, she done seed two crows! I'm gonna die!" Lee declared, "I just know it."

"You're not going to die," Willa said as she positioned herself between Lee's legs. "You've done this before, and you can do it again. It's just going to be a little harder this time. Work with me, and I'll do the best I can to help you until the doctor arrives."

"But the crows!"

"Forget about the crows, Lee, and do as I say! This is just a bigger baby than usual," Willa stated. "When you have a pain, and I tell you to push, you push, girl, as hard as you can. Do you hear me, Lee? Don't hold back."

Willa removed the dirty rags from around Lee and replaced them with the clean towels and sheets that she had brought with her.

Flies were buzzing all over the place. When one landed on Willa's nose, she looked up at Hedy in disgust. "For heaven sakes, Hedy," she said impatiently. "Get something and fan these flies."

Hedy found a piece of a cardboard box and stirred the air in front of Willa's face.

Once again, Lee's face contorted with pain.

"Push, Lee, push!" Willa shouted. From the look on Lee's face, Willa instantly surmised that Lee Duzen's problem was that she had been so thoroughly indoctrinated by Hedy, her mother-in-law, that she simply would not allow herself to have the baby.

Lee closed her legs and rolled from side to side. "I cain't push anymore, hit hurt too bad," she groaned. "I'm gonna die anyway."

Willa slapped her on the leg. "Open up, Lee!" When she didn't, Willa stood and leaned over her. "Listen to me, Lee Duzen. If you want this baby to live, you have got to help me deliver it. Believe me when I tell you that all the crows in the world have nothing to do with delivering a baby. Now push, damnit, Lee, **push**!"

Lee pushed and the baby slowly moved out of the birth canal.

"Oh Lord," Willa said. "Robert, where are you?"

Hedy, who was standing over Willa's shoulder, gave a gasp when she saw that the baby's face was covered with a bloody mask. "Saints of mercy!" Hedy cried. "It's been born with a veil over hit's face!"

"What do we do now, Hedy?" Willa whispered.

"I don't know," Hedy said backing away. "I've heerd of sich before, but I ain't ever seed it. I don't know what to do."

Miraculously, the door sprang open and Robert entered. Without a word, he went directly to the bed and proficiently slipped his finger under the membrane, lifting it off the baby's face. He then cleared the baby's airway and administered a few quick puffs of air into its lungs. The baby coughed and, after a couple of gulps, let out a wail that assured Robert he was fine.

A grin split the face of Tucker Duzen. "We be beholden to you, Doc," he said, pumping Robert's hand. "Maw says the little feller is gonna be able to tell the future, be'n born with a veil over his face and all."

"You don't say," Robert said, throwing a questioning stare at Willa.

Willa shrugged.

Leaning close to her ear, he whispered, "Do you suppose there's any chance of getting any hot water around here?"

"If you feel like hanging around for a couple of hours, you might could manage it," she answered.

Without another word, Robert rolled up his sleeves, dug in his bag for a bottle of alcohol and had Willa pour it over his hands.

Leaving Robert in the midst of issuing a few final instructions, Willa walked out into the fresh night air. She plopped down on the one remaining solid step of the run-down porch, thrust her hand beneath the heavy mane of hair that clung to her neck, and lifted it up. Letting it drop, she stretched her arms above her head, sensing the ache in every bone in her body.

The door opened. Willa moved from the steps to face the river. She had not been with or talked privately with Robert since the Sara Jane fiasco. Now she was not sure she could handle it.

After several seconds of silence, Robert said, "I can explain about Sara Jane, if you'll let me."

The impact of the day, compounded by the problems of the last few weeks, was too much to handle. Willa's body shook convulsively.

Robert took one look at her and pulled her into his arms. A torrent of tears flowed from her eyes and on to the front of his shirt. For a while, she had no control. Not only was she crying for her lonely self, she was crying for her girls and her parents because of the shame that her love for Robert had brought on them. Then for the defenseless baby that she had just helped to bring into a world that had no real future ahead of it.

"I've never willingly hurt you," he said over and over. "I know that I'm an impatient, arrogant brute. To top that off, I can be stupid from time to time, as stupid as hell. I care nothing for Sara Jane," he said. "I did nothing to encourage her attentions. I'm so very sorry that you got caught in the middle."

Before she could answer, she found his mouth on hers, signaling that as far as he was concerned, the conversation had ended. With a groan her body moved to acknowledge his. Have you no pride, Willa, her conscience demanded. Unexpectedly to them both, Willa pulled away.

"Robert," she finally managed to say, "I can't go on like this any longer. There are other aspects of this relationship that need to be ironed out, not just Sara Jane Lockwood. For starters, I want to know here and now, how you truly feel about me?" She felt his body tense. "Tell me, Robert," she whispered. "Do you love me? Tell me just this one time...."

For an instant, he was almost ready to admit, not only to himself but also to Willa, and maybe to the world, what his feelings were...and had been from the start. But a lifetime of insecurities and of living with demons held him back.

"I want you," he finally said. He closed his eyes, "I guess what I'm trying to say to you is that there is no other way but my way." He waited for Willa to answer. When she didn't, he went on. "If it's of any consequence, you have all that I have to give," he said softly.

Still Willa did not answer.

Releasing her, he rolled his shirtsleeves down. He waited for her response while holding his breath.

But Willa Sinclair had no response to make. She was not angry though she wondered why. Hadn't he just told her in so many words that she would never be good enough for him? That he wanted to keep her a dirty little secret that wasn't even a secret at all, thanks to Sara Jane. More heartbreaking was her realization that a part of her was resigned to settling for whatever he was willing to give. She knew that if she was not accepting, she'd be alone, totally alone. No other man could ever feed her soul the way he had. "Walk away," would be Mama's advice, "and don't look back." Walk away, she might, but Willa Sinclair knew that she'd always look back. Turning abruptly, Willa marched down the narrow path toward the boat.

Sighing, Robert followed her.

As she stood on the narrow dock, Willa studied Robert hesitantly picking his way down the path. He was in her territory now, and she was in command. She grinned in delight just thinking about having him at her mercy. Glancing at the evening fog that had begun to move in and lie heavily over the river, Willa bowed her head in satisfaction. If he wanted to get back to civilization, he was clearly going to have to depend on her. She lit the carbide light left by the Higgers on a post by the rickety dock and gingerly stepped into the small boat.

"Get in," she said.

Robert hesitated for several seconds before answering. "Did you say, did you say…get in?"

"Exactly."

"Why would I want to get into that thing?"

"Because *this thing,* as you put it, is our transportation down the river."

"But, there's no motor on it."

"We don't need one," she said, holding up the paddle. "Now get in, and sit here." She deliberately tapped the bench, which stretched across the width of the boat, with the wet paddle.

Backing away, Robert shook his head. "Couldn't we send for the Higgers and the motorboat? That's how I got here."

"Nope, this is your way home. Take it or leave it. I'll give you two seconds to decide. Otherwise you can spend the night with the Tuckers." Willa braced the end of the paddle against the dock, making ready to shove off. She really meant to leave him.

"Wait!" he called.

Robert cautiously slid into the wet seat. When the cold water soaked through his pants, he gave Willa a questioning look. Handing him the light, she said. "Hold this up for me and *don't* rock the boat, unless you want to take a night swim."

With dexterity, Willa dipped the blade of the paddle into the river, using long leisurely strokes, first on one side of the boat and then the other. Despite Robert's fears the boat glided with ease through the water until they reached the Holler.

Anxious to have his feet on solid ground, Robert hopped from the boat the second it bumped dry land. He stood as if frozen for several lengthy seconds before slowly stooping to stare at his shoes.

Without a comment, Willa jumped to solid ground and secured the boat. Facing him, she placed her hands on her hips and waited. Gradually, Robert raised his head and gave her a helpless look. For the first time in a long time, Willa Sinclair's sparkling laughter echoed across the Holler. In all his rumpled finery, Robert Vaughn stood ankle deep in mud.

Chapter 29
Return

The Paragould Southeastern train, dubbed the old *Bull* Moose, left Paragould, Arkansas, early in the morning in order to make it to Hornersville before lunch. After making several quick stops along the way, it clicked, clattered, and swayed rhythmically over the railroad tracks until it reached the city limits of Hornersville. The engineer gave a blast of the whistle, which, in turn, jolted the lone passenger in the red caboose into sitting upright in his seat.

Justin Rider gave his head a vigorous shake and blinked against the delirium caused by the malaria he had contracted while serving in the Philippines. After regaining his bearings, he wearily turned to face the window. His heart leaped in his chest at the sight of his hometown.

Off the train, standing at the depot and facing the main street, Justin leaned on a lamppost and hungrily drank in the sights of the small community; never expecting that something familiar could move him as strongly. In the heat of a fever, he felt a cold chill run down his spine. A realization struck him. Hornersville was just as he had left it. He had been to hell and back, but nothing here had changed. *Nothing's changed. Nothing's changed* at all echoed through his fevered brain, until he recognized that the answer to his nightly prayers during the war lay before him. The effort had been worth it, after all. Despite his Native American heritage, he realized that the sacrifice had protected something he held dear, dearer than he had dreamt possible during the horror of combat.

With a sense of personal fulfillment, Justin shouldered his duffel bag, and on rubbery legs, he headed for the Holler. When he reached the path that disappeared into the cottonwood trees, he paused and wiped his blurry eyes. The last thing he saw before collapsing into a dead faint was Pebo and old Bean rushing up to greet him. Silently, Pebo lifted his friend into his arms and, as easily as cradling a baby, carried him the rest of the way home.

In his sleep, Justin slid in and out of delirium, shaking with rigors so strong that his body convulsed. During moments of consciousness, he often jerked upright in bed and gazed wildly around the room, fearing that he had somehow failed in his duty as a warrior. On seeing Willa, and then Pebo, sitting in the corner of the room keeping a silent watch, he would calm and fall back into a feverish sleep.

Robert came and prescribed medicine. The rest of the Holler kept a quiet vigil until Willa announced that the fever had broken. For hours Justin slept as though dead. Finally the sound of Willa's voice penetrated his fuzzy senses.

"Welcome home, Jay Sky," she said softly.

Two weeks passed. At four o'clock one morning, a gaunt young man stood in the darkness of his home, staring out the window across a frosty Holler. Physically he was beginning to heal. Mentally, he knew it was going to take a while.

He heaved a frustrated sigh at not being able to sleep and slowly made his way through the darkness to the kitchen. After lighting the oil lamp sitting on the table, he turned his attention to the stove. With a poker, he stirred the coals in the cookstove, then added more wood. As he filled Bessie Rider's old tin coffeepot with water from the pump, he smiled at how his mother had considered the pump a luxury. It was, after all, the only *inside* pump in the Holler.

He added just the right amount of coffee, plus a dash of salt as his mama had always done, and placed the pot on the stove. To wait on the coffee, he seated himself at the wooden table, smooth as glass from many years of use, and reviewed in his mind what had transpired the night before with Ruby. In spite of himself, he felt guilty. Ruby, wistful-eyed Ruby, luscious, faithful Ruby had waited for him.

After a passionate session of love making, Ruby had said, "Did you know that *his* wife passed away while you were gone?"

"No, I didn't know that," Justin responded softly.

Ruby hesitated for a few seconds. "He plans on retiring soon. Can you believe it, Jay Sky?" She added as silently as possible, "He's actually asked me to marry him and move to Florida."

Despite her soft tone, Justin noted a slight tremor in her voice. He remained quiet for several moments, staring at the ceiling before rolling over and taking Ruby's face between his hands. Gazing deeply into her sapphire eyes, he said, "Ruby, Ruby," then kissed her forehead, her cheeks, her chin, the tip of her nose, and her lips.

Though it was going to be hard, the time had come to turn Ruby loose. He opened his mouth to speak, but she placed her fingers over his lips. Then her sensuous mouth parted in invitation. Justin could still see the sadness in her eyes as she skillfully awakened the only thing he would ever be able to share with her, his passion.

And so he'd said it, the fateful words, "Marry him, Ruby. You deserve it after all these years."

"Yes," she said softly. "With Maw gone, I guess it's the only thing to do."

"I'm sorry, Ruby," he continued. "Believe me I wish with all my heart that it could have been different." He had spoken truthfully. There would always be a place in his heart for Ruby.

Although he did not know it, his words broke Ruby's heart. She had waited so long just for the sight of his masculine face, the touch of his lips, his hands, the warmth of his encircling arms. Abruptly, she pulled the covers up under her chin and, with all the strength of the survivor within, shut the door to her heart and locked it forever.

Chapter 30
Storm

A long, cold winter slowly but surely drifted into spring. Then it began to rain, and continued to rain without stopping for over thirty-six hours. The expected high waters from the drainage ditches soon claimed the Holler in record time.

From inside the shack, Willa cupped her hands and yelled at Ben, "I can't hear you for the rain, Papa!"

Ben yelled back. "I said get a move on. There ain't much time left down here." A blast of icy wind nearly took his hat off his head. Grabbing it with both hands, he squashed it over his ears and cast a worried look in the direction of the ditch dump.

Willa, after taking a hurried look around to make sure she was not leaving anything of importance, jerked up the remaining box and hauled it onto the porch. Ben took the box from her and as quickly as possible slid it under the protection of a tarpaulin in the boat.

"Where in the hell do you think John is?" he asked, stepping back onto the porch.

Willa shook her head. "Down the river, I reckon. John never has had any sense when it comes to the water."

Ben gave an exasperated sigh and spit into the water lapping at the edges of the porch. "I warned him again yester'dy that this was gonna happen." He hooded his eyes with his hands to ward off the rain so he could search the Holler.

Willa quickly locked the front door of the shack and joined him on the end of the porch. They stood in silence for several moments, each wondering what they should do. Willa broke the silence with an involuntary shudder when the cold rain dribbled from the brim of the rain hat and slid down her neck. She pulled the collar around her throat, holding it with one hand, using the other to take a swipe at the hair plastered to her forehead. "If the dumb ass doesn't drown, he'll probably freeze to death in the weather." She turned to Ben. "When was the last time you saw him?"

"I reckon it wuz around two o'clock yester'dy afternoon. I figure he's really on a big'un by now and so pissy assed that he couldn't even hit the ground with his hat if he had to." Ben stomped around the porch in disgust. "Git'n the boat," he finally said. "After I get you back to the *Major Ray House*, I'll go down the river a ways and see if I can find him."

"Absolutely not, Papa!" With eyes burning with determination, Willa glared at Ben. "You're too old to even think about doing such a thing. He can drown for all I care!"

Ben had to admit what she said was true. There was a time he might have been able to brave the river, if anyone could, but not anymore.

Justin's voice pierced the storm. "Hey Ben, Willa," he called as he brought his boat alongside of the porch.

"You ain't seen John, have you boy?" Ben asked.

A look of concern crossed Justin's face. "Not since yesterday morning."

"We ain't either," Ben said. "We think he's down the river, probably at the line shack on a big'un and don't know his ass from a hole in the ground."

Justin glanced around. "How high do you suppose the water is by now?"

"Close to three feet." Ben pointed toward the sky, "And it don't look like this rain's gonna let up anyways soon, so she ain't gonna crest for a while."

Justin's brow wrinkled in concern. "If he's at the line shack, he's completely cut off from dry land. Maybe I should take a run down there."

"No! Justin Rider, you'll do no such thing."

Justin grinned. The only time Willa used his given name was when she was irritated at him.

Willa gave Justin a hard stare. "I will not allow Papa or you either to endanger your lives for the likes of him. I told Papa that John could drown first, and I mean it."

"She's right boy," Ben put in. "Promise me you won't even think about goin' down there. The water's mean, son, you know it as well as me. Sides, you ain't got all yore strength back from the last attack of that blasted fever."

"I know," Justin said. "I'll be careful."

Ben shook his head as Justin shoved the boat away from the porch. By rights he shouldn't even be out in this weather. Why that boy didn't promise me a damn thing, he thought. He didn't feel good about leaving Jay Sky behind, no sir he didn't feel good a'tal. He took his seat in his own boat but then stood up. "Remember boy," he called out, "he ain't yore responsibility . . ."

Justin threw up his hands as if to concede the point.

Willa untied the boat and jumped in, grabbed the extra paddle, and assisted Ben in propelling the boat out into the swirling current.

As the uneasiness persisted, Ben studied Willa, and then turned to stare over his shoulder in the direction of the river. Something was nagging at him. "Something keeps telling me we shouldn't leave the boy."

Willa's eyes rested on Justin's back for as long as she could see him. "I know, Papa. I feel the same way."

"Don't do it, boy," Ben whispered.

By noon, several shacks in the Holler had already succumbed to the high water.

Justin checked his cabin for the last time and climbed into the boat. He rested the paddle on his knees and tapped his fingers on the handle. He just couldn't leave without trying to find John. Taking a deep breath of courage, he paddled as swiftly as possible in the direction of the line shack, which was located near the Missouri and Arkansas State line. When he entered the river, the first thing on his mind was to stay out of the path of the tree trunks that were being yanked up by the surge of the flood. If he could avoid getting hit by something, getting to the state line would be relatively easy in the fast current. However, getting back would be near to impossible. Water had never gotten into the Sky house, and Justin didn't think it would this time. He thought if he could find John and get back to the Sky House, that they'd be safe enough until the idiot could help him paddle the boat up the river.

As Justin approached the knoll, he could hear John singing. Scrambling up the muddy bank, he yelled, "John, you stupid ass! I ought to let you drown! You useless piece of humanity." Despite being weakened, he found enough strength to take Willa's inebriated husband and unceremoniously throw him into the boat.

John wallowed around and finally pulled himself to his elbows. "Why'didn't'cha just let old John die! Hell, don't nobody give a shit about old John, so what are you doin' down here? Kiss old John's ass, Justin Rider! Just kiss old John's ass! Jus—t...kiss...oo—ld ...John's....ass!" Grabbing the gunwales of the boat for support, John pulled himself to his feet. Unfastening his belt, he downed his pants, bent over, and bared his butt for Justin's benefit. The swimming in John's head caused him to weave. The mud on his shoes plus the water in the bottom of the boat made him lose his footing.

Justin sounded a warning, but it was too late. John tumbled from the back of the boat into the swirling water.

"Hell, John!" Justin shouted in disgust. He threw himself on his knees and stretched out as fast as he could, managing to grab Willa's husband by the arm. Realizing that he lacked the strength to get John back into the boat, Justin searched his mind for a solution. Before he could react, John's violent kicking pulled Justin into the raging river.

While hanging on to John with one hand, Justin tried to grab onto the boat with the other. Before he could get a firm grip, he felt the powerful pull of the current.

Numb and exhausted, not only from the freezing river but from his illness, Justin could fight no longer. He sank into the darkness, the deep, deep darkness until he knew no more....

In a blink of an eye, the turbulent, muddy fury was gone and in its place, Justin gazed upon a river of tranquility. Wildflowers in an array of dazzling color covered the banks as far as the eye could see. As if on command, each blossom lifted its head and gently shook off crystal clear droplets of sparkling dew.

Moving in a dream like state, Justin's eyes drifted from one wondrous sight to another until he reached a tiny meadow where the dew clung and sparkled like a carpet of precious stones. He emerged from the water, dropped to his knees, and ran his hands in awe over the blades of the greenest grass that he had ever seen.

The voice of the wind called to him and bid him listen as the trees, sang in harmonious unity with the birds. How he had come to enter into this paradise of purity and perfection, he did not know, but he felt for the first time in his life the joy of unconditional acceptance.

Pulling himself to his feet, Justin faced the east, lifted his arms in an Native American appeal to the heaven, then slowly sank back to his knees as the glorified scene magically intensified to a brilliance beyond description.

"Am I in Heaven?" he asked the wind. But the wind was not at liberty to say. Instead, it crooned and caressed his brow and then with soft assuring strokes, gently turned him to face the river. The river lifted, forming a

giant mirror. Will Sky, strong and straight in the traditional ceremonial dress of his ancestors, stepped out.

All anxieties slowly slipped away as Justin Sky Rider's Native American ancestors gathered about him, each touching him with love.

The impact of hearing that Justin's abandoned boat had been found caused Willa to stagger. She clung to the door and stared wild-eyed at Ben. "Oh, dear God, Papa!" she sobbed. "Tell me what I'm hearing isn't so."

"I wish I could tell you that, Willa," Ben whispered, "I damn shore wish I could. But the truth is we figure that they both drowned."

Dropping to her knees, Willa turned to the Lord. "Please Lord," she cried, "you can't have taken Justin." Her eyes wildly searched the room as if seeking a refuge. "I just can't stand it," she muttered. "It's too damn much! I know I deserve to be punished for the life that I have led, but this?" The overwhelming desire to run, to escape from it all, swept over her. She dashed out the door and ran through the wind until she reached the edge of the backwater and stared blindly toward the empty Holler. Exhausted, she sank to the ground, wrapped her arms about her knees, and in a state of shock began to bargain with the Almighty. There she remained until Ben found her and led her away.

After putting Willa to bed, Ben and Effie sat by her bedside. "It's possible that this be the straw that broke the camel's back," Effie told Ben. Then the old blue hen bowed her head. "Lord," she prayed, "I asked you a long time ago, if it be your will, not to put on us anymore than we can tolerate. I'm askin' you this time to do the same for my girl, since she ain't able to ask for herself. Amen."

"Amen to that," Ben added.

Everyone was so caught up in their own personal grief that no one had given any thought to Pebo. If anyone had taken time to think about him, they would have realized Pebo had not been seen since he had heard about Jay Sky's boat.

Despite the danger, Pebo took old Bean, loaded him into his boat and headed for the Sky House. As he paddled down the river, he carefully scanned it for any signs of life. After securing his boat at the Sky House, Pebo opened the door, and in his haste, stumbled and nearly fell over an obstacle blocking the way. Justin Rider lay on the floor of the small cold room, barely conscious, and shivering uncontrollably.

"Please to thank you God-A-Mighty!" Pebo shouted when he saw that it was Jay Sky. "How's yore mama doin? How's yore mama doin?"

The giant, who observed the quivering mass on the floor, was able to make out but one truth: his friend was cold, very cold.

"Come on, Bean," Pebo said. Intuitively, he draped his body and that of the old dog's body over Justin Rider, forming a protective blanket. The man-child began to pray the only prayer that his impeded mind could perceive; "Now I lay me down to sleep. I pray the Lord my soul to keep."

Despite the conditions, a listless Willa returned to the edge of the water to keep the vigil. On the third day, while resting her head on her knees, seemingly urged by an unknown hand, she rose to her feet, shaded her eyes and starred at a dot on the water so far on the horizon that she could barley see it. Caught in a paralysis, she watched until she could tell by the size of the man paddling the boat that it had to be Pebo, and he was not alone.

Leaning on Pebo and Willa for support, Justin Rider was able to make his way from the boat to the temporary dwelling in the old Major Ray House. Against his protest, Willa arranged to have the doctor pay a call. Robert, looking haggard and ashen, entered the room, and without as much as a word to anyone, he placed his medical bag on the rickety table beside Justin's bed and proceeded to examine him. After a thorough check up, he declared to a proud Pebo that he had indeed saved Rider's life.

Without further ado, he snapped his medical bag shut and stood up. Pushing back his jacket, he planted his hand on his hip and said with calm authority. "You're a lucky man, Rider. You had a near-death experience and lived to tell about it. In your weakened condition," he added matter-of-factly, "it's a miracle you didn't die of hypothermia."

A near-death experience...Justin cast a glance about the dismal room and savored the words. "Yes," he finally said, "I guess I did." In more ways than one, he silently added.

A sharp pain suddenly shot through Robert's chest. Dropping his medical bag, he sank back into the chair, grabbed the corner of the small table for support, and clutched at his heart.

Willa took a step toward him. Reaching out, she placed her hand on his arm. "Robert, what is it?" She quizzed.

"It's nothing to concern yourself about," he answered in an abrupt but noticeably unsteady voice. Shaking off her hand, he managed to pull himself to his feet.

Willa reached down in front of him, retrieved his medical bag lying on its side and handed it to him. When he took it from her, she noted a slight trembling in his hand. Not meeting her eyes, he said, "Make sure he gets plenty of rest," and then turned slowly on his heels and left the room.

Visibly upset by the turn of events, Willa's questioning gaze sought Justin's. He nodded his head in acquiescence.

Exhausted, Robert returned to the office. He tried to shake off the ache that had settled in his arm and chest, but when he couldn't, he was forced to lie down. In less than five minutes, Willa entered through the back door, took one look at him and saw that he was suffering despite his will to hide it. She canceled all further appointments for the afternoon.

"Do you have medicine that I can get you for this illness?" She asked him.

"Who said I was ill?" He growled.

Willa placed her hand on her hips. "Well then, do you have any medicine that I can get you for this illness that you don't have?" Several seconds passed. "I'm waiting," she announced.

"Yes," he finally said. "It's in my bag." She couldn't help but note the edge of impatience that underlined his every word.

After administering the pill to Robert, Willa stared at the bottle that she held in her hand. *For congenital heart disease*, the prescription read. Her throat tightened as every fiber in her being screamed at the term *congenital.* From personal experience, it was a term that she knew well. With the pain of the past put from her mind, she hovered over him and asked, "Is there anything I can do to help?"

"All I want from you is to be left alone," he muttered.

"That I will not do, so you might as well get ready to talk to me," she declared as she pulled up a nearby chair. "I'm not leaving here until you explain to me what this means?"

Robert emptied the glass that she had given him and then set it aside. After wiping the sheen of perspiration from his forehead, he rested his elbows on his knees and clasped his hands.

From his own lips, Willa learned the terrifying truth and her head reeled from it. Tears pricked her eyes. He looked so vulnerable, so frail that she suddenly wanted to protect him, but she dared not touch him. Instead, she took a deep breath, fought back the tears and tried to question him further. He grew impatient. "A legacy from my mother," was all he was willing to impart. Willa wasn't so sure about that.

Later that evening after feeding the girls, Willa left the Major Ray House and walked aimlessly through the streets of the town desperately searching her mind for answers. Soon she was sitting on the steps of the First Baptist Church, located across the street from the rooming house. The grief she felt for Robert welled up so painfully inside of her that she thought she would burst with agony.

She kept asking herself, in bargaining with the Almighty, had she unwittingly bargained Robert's life for Justin's? Finally, she pulled herself to her feet, took a deep breath of courage and opened the door to the church and entered it for the first time. There, she beseeched God with all her heart that she had not been guilty of committing this horrible action. The question that haunted her as she prayed was, did she dare bargain for the man she loved with all her heart?

Chapter 31
On the Demise

After Justin Rider's return, a party of men was assembled to search the still swollen river for John Sinclair's body. From time to time the eerie sound of gunfire could be heard, an effort prompted by the old belief that a body lying on the bottom could be brought to the surface by the report of a gun.

When the river eventually relinquished the body of John Sinclair, Ben asked the Reverend Johnson, who held a bi-weekly service under the cottonwood tree, to preach John's funeral.

The good Reverend, in an attempt to gather a few kind words to use in John's eulogy, canvassed the Holler. When he couldn't find anyone who would offer any suggestions, he approached Ben and Effie Melton.

Ben stiffened. Effie could be artlessly blunt, and no one knew it better than he did. For Effie, there was no good to be found in John. As far as she could tell, dying didn't make him any better a man. Without mincing her words, Effie looked the preacher straight in the eye and asked, "Do you want to know the long and the short of it, Preacher?"

"Of course, Mrs. Melton, of course," he answered, shaking all four chins. The good reverend leaned in and so did Effie.

"Don't feel bad, Preacher, 'cause it ain't yore fault," she soothed, "but thar ain't nothin' good you can possibly say before God about John and tell the truth. I'm accust'm to telling the truth and so are you. So I'm going to tell you just like it is. He weren't nothin' but a pissy ass drunk!"

Days later, while standing on the dump facing the water, Ben took a can of Prince Albert tobacco from his overall pocket, dumped a narrow line onto the thin white paper he held in his other hand, and then with thumb and forefinger expertly rolled it into a cigarette. He licked and smoothed it, struck a match on the seat of his pants, bent his head to his cupped hands, and lit the end of the cigarette. Flipping the match into the river, he swiped at a fly crawling on his nose and removed a lose bit of tobacco from his tongue. Despite a tremendous effort to control his feelings, Ben Melton shed a single tear down his lined cheeks. He stared at the river. The river had been his life. No one knew any better than he the way of things on the river. It throbbed with life and death, giving and taking.

A short distance away, Vernie and Mernie Higgers sat on the front porch watching as Pebo cleaned the grounds around their houses. After tossing an armload of debris onto a burning pile, Pebo paused to examine a small laceration in his right thumb. Ben watched with interest as Pebo, holding his thumb out like a small child, ran to the porch.

"Let me see yore thumb," Vernie told him. Reaching behind her, she grabbed a jug and doused the cut with coal oil. After ripping a scrap of cloth from the drying rag hanging on the porch, she patted Pebo's arm. "There," she stated, "that ought to keep it clean."

Old Bean awoke and ambled over to where Ben was, and affectionately licked his hand. After patting the old dog and scratching his head, Ben took a deep breath and glanced around. As far as places to live were concerned, he guessed the Holler was the pits. But at the present, it didn't seem all that bad to him.

It's funny, he thought, how much smarter the Lord lets an old man get just before it's time for him to fold his tent and move on to a better place. He'd never been able to make any sense of the fact that some people were called so early in life, especially the little ones like baby Ben, his grandson. But at least for today, it all seemed to make perfect sense. He didn't know if he could put words to his feelings, but suddenly he felt he sort'a understood what this old life was all about. Time never stops, even when someone breathes his or her last breath. No matter how good, how rich, how poor, at what age, or how much they are loved, there would always be a tomorrow for some folks, and for others, today would be their last. The cycle would repeat itself day after day until it was all over. What it all amounts to, he decided, is that no matter what happens to you in this life, don't take it personal, cause it ain't meant that way. He reckoned if he told Jay Sky what he was thinking, he would have a name for it.

Ben dropped his cigarette and ground it out with his foot. As he turned to go home, the droop was gone from his shoulders. He guessed everything happened for the best. It all rests in the hands of God and rightly so. If he lived to the morrow, he reckoned he and his family would be moving out of the Holler.

As Ben walked toward home, the winds of change returned and blew over him once again, disguised as a light breeze.

Effie had been watching her husband from the back porch of the shack. "Are you alright?" she asked.

"Yep, I reckon I am, better'n I've been in a long time." With that he patted her shoulder, stepped past her, and gingerly walked into the shack.

Effie shook her head at the turn of events. She took a deep breath and blew out a little cloud of white fog from the coolness of the evening. She rose and reached to open the back door. Pausing, she wrapped her arms in her apron tail and let her gaze wander from one weathered shack to another. She was moved by the soft glow of lamplight in the windows.

Bleakness came into her dark eyes. Such as it was, it had been home to her for most of her life. "There's a time and place to do all things," she said. "I reckon you're right, Ben. It's time for us to move on."

Chapter 32
Without End

The tick of the clock, the rain dripping from the eaves of the house and the labored snoring of the lone man lying on a recliner in the dark room produced a rhythmic tempo. His sleep was disturbed when a sharp pain in his chest shot him awake.

Not giving the pain or its effect a second thought, he simply reached into the pocket of his rumpled shirt for the tiny brown bottle of pills. When the pain ceased, he searched the contents on the table beside him for his small gold pocket watch. Flipping open the case, he studied it, then nodded his head in satisfaction with the early morning hour. He still had enough time to do what needed to be done.

"It's time we put an end to this madness," he said trying to renew an old acquaintance. "Don't you agree, Lord?" Having been raised as a Catholic, he made the sign of the cross and whispered. "Father, forgive me for I have sinned." He wondered if it would be necessary to enumerate them specifically? After careful consideration, he decided they were too numerous to mention. "Excuse me a moment," he said. Pulling himself to his feet, he slowly made his way to the bathroom to shower and shave. Returning to the study, he dropped into the overstuffed chair, laid his head back, and closed his eyes. When he heard the kitchen door open, he smiled. "Where were we, Lord?" he said softly.

Normally Willa tried not to disturb Robert, but since she had not seen him for several days, she was worried. Walking to the door of the study, she listened for any sound he might make. On the other side of the door, without her being aware of it, he was listening as carefully as she was.

The self-imposed isolation had given Robert the time he needed to think. After careful consideration, he had summoned James Shaw and completed his Last Will and Testament. He sincerely hoped that he had done the right thing.

"A man's character is molded while he is young," he had told James. "My regret is that I was weak. I could have overcome my problems; instead, I wallowed in self-pity."

Listening for any motion Willa might make, he reflected on the last few years. I have no one to blame but myself, he thought. I had a chance to do differently, but I chose to cleave to my ways, and it cost me dearly.

Willa, meanwhile, busied herself putting away the items from the basket that she brought with her. "I'm tired of playing cat and mouse," she told the plant that still graced the window. "If I don't hear something from him by the time I feed you, I'll march right down that hall and pound on the door." Without a doubt, any forwardness on her part would bring on a tirade of language not fit for anyone's ears. Robert's pain had made him testy of late.

"Is that you, woman?"

The unexpected sound of his voice caused Willa to jump. She walked to the door of the study. "You know it is."

"Come in here," he said.

Willa opened the door and waited until her eyes adjusted to the dimness of the room. "From the looks of this room, it's about time you let me in here," she said. Picking up a book from the floor, she returned it to a bookshelf. "What's happened to you?" she asked. "You used to be so neat." Even in the darkness, she felt his eyes following her.

"Leave things alone, Willa," he said softly, "and come here. I want to talk to you."

With an exasperated sigh, Willa turned to face him. "But there's so much to do in…." Their eyes locked, and for several long seconds, they stared at each other.

"Come here, Willa, and sit down beside me," he said in a whisper.

She shook her head, "No. No, Robert, I won't do it. I can't do it." She grabbed a pillow from the sofa and plumped it. Snatching up a pile of newspapers, she frantically tried to stuff them into an overflowing wastebasket.

"You know," she said, trying to ward off the inevitable, "I believe that I actually heard you call me Willa. What happened to Mrs. Sinclair?"

"Willa," he admonished, "leave the damn stuff alone and come over here and sit down."

Willa froze, closed her eyes, and slowly let the papers slide to the floor. Moving like a zombie, she crossed the room, dropped to her knees in front of him. "No, Robert, no," she pleaded. "I don't want to hear it." Burying her face into his chest, she began to sob, heart breaking sobs that were torture to his ears. "With God as my witness, Robert," she declared, before sucking in a great gulp of air. "If I could make you whole again, or if I could just prolong your life by giving you part of mine, I would do it. I've even prayed to do it." She wailed in anguished.

Wrapping his arms around her, he cradled her to him. Rocking her as gently as a baby. "My darling, my darling," he crooned. "Please don't shed anymore tears for me. I don't deserve them." An anguished sigh escaped his lips. "You would have been better off if I had never come into your life."

"Please don't say that," she moaned.

Robert closed his eyes against the pain of so many wasted years. When he opened them, his lashes were wet with tears. "You asked me a long time ago to tell you how I feel about you," he whispered. "I was a coward, so I didn't, and I have lived to regret it."

As Willa opened her mouth to speak, he placed his fingers over her lips. Shaking his head from side to side, he softly said, "Let me finish...I love you, Willa."

With that simple admittance, for the first time in his life, Robert Vaughn threw open the gates of his heart. Years of pent-up emotion and love gushed out soothing Willa's aching heart. "You know, I think that I have loved you from the first day I saw you in my office wearing that god-awful hat."

Smiling through her tears, Willa tried without much success to feign indignation. "I happen to have loved that hat," she said weakly.

Robert chuckled and kissed the top of her head. After a long silence, he said. "There's one more sin, I need to atone for. Being the most important one, I saved it for last." He took a deep breath. "I've always known that Gensi's my child. I am so very, very sorry for my actions toward her. Can you forgive me?"

Willa touched the tears on his cheek. "Yes, my love," she whispered, "I forgive you."

With her head on his chest, Willa could hear the uneven beats of his faint and struggling heart. Life was slowly slipping away from the love of her life, and she could do nothing to stop it.

Knowing that she would never leave on her own, Robert caught her face between his hands. Kissing her lips, he pushed her from him and said, "I want you to go now and don't come back until you hear from James Shaw."

Willa opened her mouth to protest. Knowing that any objection that she might make would stress him, she decided against it. Rising to her feet, she reluctantly walked to the door.

Though Robert knew that the offer he was about to make was purely symbolic, he felt a compelling need to do it. "One more thing, Willa," he said, as he shifted his position in the chair, trying, without making it obvious, to hide the disturbing sensation that was settling in his body.

Willa's hand clenched around the doorknob before she turned to face him. Their eyes met and held.

"I want you to know that deep down, it has always been my heart's desire…"

"Yes, Robert?" She whispered.

"Will you marry me?"

Willa realized that she had been holding her breath and softly exhaled. She opened the door, leaned her head against it and closed her eyes. Turing to face him, she said, "Yes, I'd like that. I'd like that very much." With a bittersweet smile, she threw him a kiss and walked backwards through the door, gently closing it behind her.

The rest of the day passed into night without word from James Shaw. Around midnight, Willa crawled into her bed. Knowing there would be no sleep for her, she propped herself against the pillows and waited alone in the dark room…until she knew in her heart that Robert Vaughn's life had slipped away.

Epilogue

Over the years, unbeknownst to anyone other than James Shaw, Robert Vaughn had added to his fortune by improving upon and then selling Dr. Wilson's many remedies to a pharmaceutical company.

In his Will, Vaughn left the bulk of his estate to his daughter Gensi, and a considerable sum of money to Will. He attached one condition, that the girl's mother openly proclaims the child's paternity. Since Sarah Jane Lockwood had already made the affair public, James Shaw had no difficulty in convincing a probate judge that the Will should be executed as written. The generosity of the payment, in addition to the Will's liberal language, allowed Willa to exercise control over the money and use it equally for the benefit of Aster, Gensi's half sister. Thereby, Willa Sinclair became the richest person in southeast Missouri and was given the freedom to determine her own future, if somewhat belatedly.

The early loss of her lover made her aware of her own mortality, and she retained James Shaw to draw up her own Will. In it, she divided her inheritance equally between her two daughters, except for one precious atomizer and matching tray, which was eventually to pass into the hands of Gensi Sinclair Vaughn.

About the Author

Jewette Battles writes with an insight of her birthplace on the banks of Little River in the Southeast Missouri bootheel. Now residing in Kosciusko, Mississippi, with her husband Tom, Jewette is working on a sequel to *The Blue Hen's Chicken*

Printed in the United States
2482

9 780595 126781